LOST CONTACT
Mystery Novel

Joan Carson

CrownPeak
PUBLISHING

This is a work of fiction. All of the characters, organizations, and events portrayed in this novel are either products of the author's imagination or are used fictitiously.

LOST CONTACT

ISBN-13: 978-0-9645663-8-5
ISBN-10: 0-9645663-8-9

Library of Congress Control Number: 2012953842

Editors: Paula L. Silici & Donna Jackson
Literary Agent: Donna Jackson
Cover Art by Kent Jackson
Layout Design by Ann Ramsey

Published by
Crown Peak Publishing
PO Box 317
New Castle, CO 81647
www.crownpeakpublishing.com

First Edition

Printed in the United States of America

FOR STEPHEN
who inspires me and stands by me

Acknowledgments

First and foremost, to my friend, Pamela Curtiss, who began this project with me and has helped with editing and creative suggestions throughout the process.

I cannot fully express my gratitude to my husband, Stephen Schoepflin, and my brother, James Stadler, who had exceptional input with the plot and character development of *Lost Contact*. My family and friends have been very supportive and I appreciate all their encouragement. Thank you especially to my agent, Donna Jackson, and editor, Paula L. Silici, for their wonderful guidance, inspiration and talents for polishing and "tightening and brightening" this story. And finally, for the artistic talents of my publisher and graphic designer, Ann Ramsey, and the illustrator, Kent Jackson, who created a stunning book cover, thank you.

LOST CONTACT

PROLOGUE

Taking full advantage of his last day in Aspen, Jack Kelly got up early to be the first to ski down the challenging Face of Bell run. The sky was brilliant blue on this Saturday morning, late February, and a foot of soft snow had fallen the night before. This "knee deep in champagne powder" phenomenon occurred at only a few places on earth and brought the rich and famous to Aspen, Colorado, every year.

Few skiers distracted him as he expertly crisscrossed among the trees. He skied all day with no break for lunch. As the mountain consumed him, he temporarily forgot about the problems that overwhelmed his life and career—his shady business partner, a pending civil lawsuit, and a possible criminal investigation.

As the cold snow brushed his face, he finally understood what his course of action had to be.

CHAPTER 1

Lauren found Jack in a secluded area of the airport talking on a cell phone, speaking in whispered tones as if the conversation were secret and private. She didn't mean to eavesdrop, but her curiosity got the best of her. As she edged behind him, she heard Jack say, "Believe me, I'm trustworthy. I'll meet you on Monday, three o'clock, as we previously arranged." He dropped his cell phone into his jacket pocket, and when he turned around, collided with Lauren. She tried to hide her embarrassment at being caught so obviously listening to his conversation. He reacted like a cornered animal, grabbing her by the arms and glaring at her.

"Were you spying on me?" he demanded. "Are you a reporter? Who are you working for?"

With his muscular body pressed so tightly against hers, she could tell he was still in great physical shape. "No, no, Jack. I'm with the airport," she managed to say. "I've been trying to find you. Your charter plane needs to depart, that's all. One of the other passengers has a tight connection at Denver International Airport. You haven't answered your pages. I recognized your name and figured I could find you if you were anywhere in the airport."

"Oh," he said, his taut features relaxing. Jack still had that sparkle in his blue eyes, although she could tell that something was weighing heavily on his mind. She wondered what she might have overheard that would cause such a strong reaction. Even though she was used to dealing with angry passengers—some she thought might become violent—being grabbed in that manner unnerved her. She struggled to recover her composure.

"You obviously don't remember me," she said as she tried to lighten the mood. "We dated in college. I'm Lauren—Lauren Reese. You used to come to my house—my parents' house here in Aspen, on Waters Avenue. Do you remember? I recently inherited the home and I live alone there now."

Her long brown hair was pulled back away from her face with a stylish scarf, so she understood why he probably didn't recognize her. He loosened his grip and carefully studied her. As he dropped his hands to his side, he apologized for his rough reaction.

"Sorry. I'm under a lot of stress right now. I do remember you," he finally said, smiling slightly. "Yes, the house on Waters. How could I forget?"

"No problem. I didn't mean to sneak up on you. I work here as an assistant airport administrator, and part of my job is finding errant passengers. Listen. You need to get moving. Really—your plane is ready to take off."

"Okay, I'll grab my things. Tell the pilot I'll meet them at the gate." He started to turn away.

Not wanting him to rush off, Lauren quickly asked, "By the way, how's your dad?"

His expression turned sullen again. "He's in an assisted living facility. He has dementia, possibly Alzheimer's, and some physical limitations which keep him from living on his own."

"Really? I'm sorry to hear that. He's so young to be in that condition," Lauren said with real concern. She remembered Rick Kelly as a fun and caring man—very strong, determined and balanced with a great sense of humor.

"How are your parents?"

Lauren felt her face go pale as she replied, "They were in a fatal car accident about a year and a half ago. And as I've just mentioned, I live in their house here in Aspen now. Things were really rough for a while, but I'm finally getting settled."

"I'm so sorry," he said, and then, "We have a lot to talk about. It seems like way too much has happened since we last saw each other. I wish I had run into you sooner. Maybe next time I'm here we could get together—catch up. What has it been? Over ten years? More like twelve or fifteen, I guess."

"That sounds about right."

She looked at the ruggedly handsome man in front of her. His brown hair was a little longer than one might expect from a successful Harvard-educated businessman, and his face was weathered from a week of skiing. She momentarily forgot about his scandalous reputation.

"Yes, I would love that," she said, and meant it. She smiled at him and then left to inform the pilot that Jack was on his way. After a few moments, she turned and watched as he headed down the hall toward his flight.

She smiled again as she thought about how seeing him for just those few moments had awakened dormant feelings in her, warm, romantic feelings. Warm feelings on a cold winter day.

Why did I have to run into Jack just when he was leaving Aspen? It had bothered her through the years that he no longer kept in touch. She'd held a small flame for him in the back of her heart all this time.

And how could it have been over twelve years since she'd seen him? Where had those years gone? She had spent so much time working on her career that her personal life was empty. She was finally ready to focus on developing a serious relationship. She had dated several men since Jack, but none had any special meaning. Maybe she and Jack could have a second chance. He'd said he would contact her the next time he was in town and there was still plenty of time before the ski season ended. At least that was something to look forward to. He seemed pleased to see her again. *Could he tell the feeling was mutual?*

3

CHAPTER 2

What a day! thought Lauren Reese as she pulled her Jeep Cherokee up to the front of her quaint, mountain home. She walked into her refurbished two-bedroom house and hung her scarf and plush brown wool coat on pegs by the door. She noticed her skis standing against the wall as she took off her boots and wished she had more time to enjoy her favorite sport.

It had been one of those Saturdays. They were always a challenge at the local Sardy Field Regional Airport, and this one was no exception. Aspen was too far from Denver to be a commuter ski area, so visitors typically stayed from Saturday to Saturday. This Saturday, though, the excellent snow conditions had resulted in an overbooked ski resort, which meant she had to deal with hundreds of travelers. On top of that, she'd had a brief encounter with Jack Kelly.

She'd dated Jack when they attended the University of Colorado in Boulder, which seemed like ages ago. They'd hung out with the same crowd and often skied together during their breaks. Jack's father Rick was the beloved football coach at CU, which made the family an icon in the popular university town. Rick Kelly was also a friend of the Reese family and had been a mentor to Lauren's cousin Eric when Eric had gotten in with the wrong crowd at college. He'd been losing track of his academic goals, partying too much, and the Kelly family suggested he try out for the football team since he had played in high school. Rick had taken Eric under his wing and taught him how to be successful, both on and off the field. He'd taken time to care, and for that, the Reese family would be forever grateful. Eric graduated and now worked for a large accounting firm in downtown Denver.

Seeing Jack made Lauren think back to a time of innocence and anticipation of bright futures with no limitations when they met at the C.U. ski club. Jack had graduated with a business degree and then moved on to earn an MBA from Harvard Business School. After graduation, they'd kept in touch for a while, but the distance between Boston and Colorado proved to be too much for their relationship. It had been a few years since she'd heard from him. She had, however, read about him occasionally in the alumni newsletter. He was currently vice president of Last Defense, a private security government contractor firm based out of Houston—a business whose employees were known as "covert government mercenaries."

Recently, Lauren had read in the newspaper that Jack's company was being sued by the family of one of its employees who had been killed in Afghanistan. The family believed circumstances surrounding the death of their son were extraordinary. They felt he had been placed in a dangerous location, and the suit alleged that Last Defense should have known to avoid the area. Now the family members were seeking compensation for the loss of their son, even though in exchange for a high rate of compensation, he signed a contract relieving the company of any liability in case of death or dismemberment in the course of performing his job duties.

It seemed to Lauren that Harvard and Last Defense had changed Jack into a hard nose businessman who only cared about money. She'd also heard about his playboy escapades from college friends who lived in Houston where Jack now resided. She was somewhat dismayed when she heard about his latest love interests—or as she saw it, conquests. He may have been her type in college, but not now. She had grown up, but apparently he had not, or so she thought.

Too tired to make dinner, Lauren poured herself a glass of wine and opened a prepackaged salad, devouring it quickly, as there had been no time for lunch during her busy workday. Sitting at her kitchen table, she looked fondly out at her living room, which was decorated with a warm, bright, red wool Navajo rug that lay over a portion of the refinished hardwood floor. On the walls hung Southwestern-style artwork she had purchased in Winter Park and Santa Fe. A leather chair and sofa surrounded an oak coffee table, and along the far wall a curio cabinet housed handmade Indian pots.

It hadn't been easy to decorate the house after the untimely death of her parents. She wanted a more modern look than what they had been fond of. She'd painted the front room a warm beige that accented the bright colors of her newly found paintings, when she'd finally decided to accept that living in Aspen would be best for her. Now she found her home a safe haven after stressful days at work.

Walking over to her bookcase, she took out a photo album of her days in college. She found a picture of Jack and herself right away. Her fingertips caressed the picture as she remembered that magical time in her life. When she'd run into Jack today, it didn't look like he had changed much. Had she? She smiled as she looked through the other pictures in the album. They all brought back cherished memories of an innocent, playful, and carefree time in her life.

She shivered slightly and felt a chill in the air. Checking the stack of wood near the fireplace, she decided there was enough to make a small fire tonight. Placing chunks of wood in the hearth, she shoved some twisted newspaper in the cracks, and held a lighter to it. The fire started with a few crackles and snaps. Lauren stared at the flames, the heat assaulted her face but felt wonderfully warm.

One of the benefits she'd found of having her own house was being able to do whatever she wanted at any given time. Deciding to spend the rest of the evening relaxing in front of the fire, she stretched out on her comfortable leather sofa, wrapped herself up in a warm blanket, and turned on the television. The program became background noise as she reflected on the events of the day and the array of emotions she found herself feeling from her encounter with Jack.

Well, the day was over and she was thoroughly exhausted. The airport had been busier than usual, and all she could think about was a nice, hot, massaging shower and then a good book to read until she fell asleep. She was looking forward to skiing on her day off tomorrow.

Suddenly, a blaring TV news bulletin startled her out of her reverie.

"**Breaking News**—*a small private charter jet that left Aspen Sardy Field airport at 4:10 this afternoon has lost contact with ground control and possibly crashed. It is believed that an executive from Hewlett Packard and Jack Kelly, a Colorado native and son of Rick Kelly, former coach of the CU Buffs were among the passengers. Stay tuned for further details.*"

CHAPTER 3

Lauren couldn't believe her eyes and ears as she stared at the television. Was it possible that Jack had just been killed? Air traffic controllers had lost contact with his plane, and it wasn't looking good. She lowered her face into her hands. That just wouldn't be fair, to have found her old love, even it was for just a moment, and then have him disappear forever. There were so many things she'd wanted to catch up on and share with him. How could that no longer be possible? And what would happen to Jack's dad?

But she was getting ahead of herself. Planes often lost contact with controllers while flying in the mountains. That didn't mean the plane had crashed. Why was the media making such a big deal about this missing plane?

She sighed heavily, remembering how her hopes were crushed when she lost her parents. She'd been close to her mother, and was becoming closer to her emotionally distant father when both had met their untimely deaths. She had been working at Denver International Airport as an assistant to the general manager of operations. A convoluted title, but basically she'd done some of the same work she was doing now, but on a larger, more specific scale. Nothing to hold her in Denver, she moved into the Aspen home that her parents had been residing in.

They had moved there from Denver at the beginning of her freshman year at Colorado University in Boulder. Although the family had owned the house for years, it had been rented out while Lauren and her sister went through school. The empty nest gave her parents an opportunity to sell their home and move to Aspen.

Reminiscing brought Lauren to a startling conclusion. Reflecting on her past relationships, she realized the only time she did feel unconditional love was with Jack.

The grandfather clock over the fireplace mantel chimed nine times, and Lauren realized she was too mentally and physically exhausted to think about those things anymore. Time for that hot massaging shower she'd promised herself. It would relax her and help her to psychologically deal with the events of the day and the latest news about the missing plane. She would need all of her energy to handle the chaos at work the next day. Which reminded her, no one from work had called so, maybe the plane had been found and she could enjoy her day off tomorrow, or, more likely, there was so much going on at the airport that no one had time to call her. Either way, her personal feelings would have to be put on hold while she dealt with the responsibilities of her job and a good night's sleep would help, too.

Opening the package of soothing lavender soap from the grief support group she'd attended after losing her parents, she questioned why she felt sad. After all, she hadn't seen Jack in years. Maybe she was mourning the loss of hopeful romance with a lost love. It all seemed to end before it had the chance to begin again.

Aromatherapy had been one of many ways she'd pampered herself after losing her parents and she counted on the technique to help her now. The hot massaging spray felt good on her back and neck muscles tight from stress and anxiety. After a few minutes, her whole body began to relax. Thoughts about the news report echoed in her brain. No question, she would have to work tomorrow. The public relations nightmare of a missing plane after leaving Aspen would be trying. Worse, yet, the missing plane also involved a personal tragedy. Taking a deep breath, she tried to focus on the warmth and comfort of the hot water enveloping her and the soothing aroma of the lavender soap.

Suddenly, she froze. A noise beyond the bathroom door took her breath away. *My God, on top of everything that has happened today, am I now being robbed?* Had she forgotten to lock the front door when she came in, or worse, had she left the keys in the door? Then she remembered that her sister often came to visit from Denver. Shannon was an avid skier and most likely couldn't pass up the great snow conditions. But Shannon usually called first, especially since Aspen was a long drive from Denver. All these thoughts raced through her mind as her heart beat loudly in her chest. Turning off the water, she strained to hear anything coming from beyond the bathroom door. Nothing. She only heard the sound of her racing pulse and the water dripping into the tub. Maybe her imagination was getting the best of her. She dried off, put on her knee-length black satin nightgown, and threw on the matching robe. In her haste, she forgot to fasten the tie. Taking a deep breath, she quietly made her way into the living room, wondering if it was a smart idea to confront whatever or whoever was making the noise.

Jack stood by the fireplace, larger than life. Speechless, she was both astonished and relieved to see him. She had forgotten how handsome he was until she saw him in the light of the soft flames. With his brown leather jacket, dark blue turtleneck sweater, jeans, and boots, he looked like something out of a dream.

Jack stood still, struck by her beauty and not wanting to alarm her further. He remembered the excitement he'd felt about her back in college and noticed she'd only gotten more beautiful. Finally he said, "I'm sorry if I frightened you."

"I heard something. I thought my sister had come by."

"I knocked but there was no answer and the door was unlocked." He couldn't take his eyes off her, thinking about how to cautiously put into words all that he wanted to tell her, knowing that he couldn't reveal everything. He caught a faint scent of lavender and relaxed a little. She looked lovely with her long dark hair tumbling past her shoulders, and her bright brown eyes captivated him. Through her open robe he could see her cleavage as her nightgown clung to her soft breasts and firm thighs.

She saw him staring and quickly tied the belt of her robe. She spoke to bring his eyes back up to her face. "You didn't make the plane," she said.

"I had a strange, weird feeling as I walked to the tarmac. I hadn't eaten all day, and I've been under tremendous stress. I felt weak and started to have chest pains. When I got on the plane, I found my seat and buckled in, but before it took off I realized it would be better for me and the other passengers if I took a later flight to Denver. I told the pilot, then grabbed my duffel bag and left. Now, I've found out that the plane has lost contact. I just saw the news report on the television at the airport." Jack looked as if he was in shock. "I'm sorry about coming here, but I didn't know where else to go."

Suddenly, Lauren realized that she wasn't being very hospitable. "Please sit down," she said as calmly as she could, motioning toward the sofa. "I'm glad you came here and that you remembered where I live. Are you feeling better now? Can I get you something to eat?"

"I ate at the airport after I got off the plane and I feel much better now, thanks. I guess it was just a panic attack brought on by stress and not enough food and sleep."

"How about something to drink? Would a glass of wine calm your nerves?"

"A glass of wine would be nice."

Lauren took two wine glasses down from the cupboard in the kitchen and uncorked a new bottle of wine. She slowly filled each glass. Walking back into the living room, she handed one to Jack. He'd taken off his jacket and was sitting on the sofa in front of the fire. He looked a bit more at ease after finally settling in a warm, friendly, safe place. She sat across the coffee table from him in her overstuffed leather chair, set down her glass, and looked at him evenly. *Why is he here?*

He seemed to read her thoughts. "I might be in trouble," he said as he sipped his wine. "I think someone's trying to kill me and I have suspicions about the missing plane. Will you help me?"

Stunned, Lauren didn't answer right away. "What's going on?" she finally asked after taking a slow sip of wine. She didn't want to commit to anything, not knowing the full story. His reputation preceded him, and she knew she had to be wise and cautious about any future involvement with him.

Jack told her about the lawsuit and then shared his deepest concern. "I don't know how far Michael Dodson, my business partner, will go to keep himself and the company out of hot water. He wants to fight the lawsuit, using all our resources to do it, and he refuses to cooperate with the investigation. He won't listen to me and has threatened me with God only knows what harm if I don't go along with his plan. I just want to find out what really happened in Afghanistan. On Monday I'm supposed to meet with a witness, Paul Johnson, who has important information he wants to share. Paul has been evasive and will only talk with me. I would be going against legal advice to meet with him, since he could be a witness for the other side."

"Do you think maybe your imagination is getting the best of you? Planes lose contact all the time here in the mountains."

"I know. I used to live here in Colorado, remember? But I just have a terrible feeling about this one."

"Surely you don't think your business partner, this Michael Dodson, would have anything to do with the missing plane?"

"I'm not so sure. He's turned into a pretty ruthless guy. He's already threatened me, as I mentioned. If he found out about my meeting with Paul Johnson, and if he thinks Johnson's information could destroy the company and his reputation, it's possible. So, I think it would be better if some people thought I was on that plane, at least for right now, until I find out more information about what happened."

"I guess I don't completely understand. Why are you fighting your business partner on this? What's in it for you? Wouldn't it be better to just let the lawyers handle it?"

He reflected for a moment, his gaze mirroring his sincerity. "I guess, like the plane, I've lost contact with my conscience. It's time to reconnect with it."

CHAPTER 4

Lauren had mixed feelings about what to do with this conflicted man for whom she used to have a romantic attachment. She wanted to help Jack, but her suspicions kept her from fully believing the story he had told. Should she let him hide out at her house so that it would appear he'd been on the plane? How bad was his situation, really? Could he be trusted? After mulling things over a few minutes, old feelings of love and admiration won out, and she decided to offer any assistance she could, telling herself it was mostly on behalf of Jack's dad that she did so.

"What can I do to help?" she asked, sipping her glass of wine, then placing it on the coffee table in front of her and folding her hands in her lap.

"I don't want to disrupt your life and put you into a dangerous situation. If you'd just let me stay here for a while, I can try to figure out whom I can trust to either meet with or at least contact the witness, Johnson, on Monday. I would contact him myself, but I think my phone and email must be hacked. It would be best if, for right now, no one knows that I wasn't on that plane."

"Who could that someone be? How can you possibly know whom you can trust? If the plane was sabotaged, either someone who knows the group you were traveling with or someone who was at the Aspen airport must have done it." She shuddered at the thought of anyone resorting to murdering innocent people—if that was what happened.

"That's true. A terrible thought, but true."

In spite of her hesitations, Lauren blurted out, "Let me go to Houston in your place and meet with the witness."

Startled, Jack shook his head. "That would be way too dangerous, I could never ask . . ."

"I'm volunteering. I insist." Now that she'd committed herself, she couldn't very well back down.

"Why would you want to do this, Lauren?"

"For your dad. I owe him. He helped our family when he became a mentor to my cousin."

"Really? What do you mean?"

"My cousin, Eric, got in with the wrong crowd his first year of college at CU. Your dad encouraged him to play football and helped straighten him out. That was exactly what my cousin needed to give him confidence and direction. He finished school, and now he's working as a CPA for a Denver firm."

"I remember Eric. I think I met him one time here, at a dinner after skiing."

Jack smiled as he thought about his dad, the infamous football coach, admired as much for his integrity as for his coaching ability.

"Thanks. My dad would appreciate it," he said. "He always believed in doing the right thing, no matter what the personal cost." Sadness washed over him as he recalled how his dad had always been so supportive of his endeavors. He really missed being able to ask for his dad's advice, and he sure could use it now.

But back to reality and the problems at hand. At first glance, Jack thought Lauren might be a good choice to represent him in Houston. He knew she'd gotten her degree in communications, and her job at the airport must require some amount of accountability and honesty. She was definitely someone he could trust. At this point he really had no other options.

"If you're serious about doing this, I can fly you out to Houston and put you up in the best hotel. I will spare no expense," he said, trying to show his full appreciation for her help. And then he hesitated. "What about taking time off from your job? Will that be difficult to arrange? When do you think you could leave?"

Lauren warmed to the idea. "Everything will be fine. I've earned vacation and accumulated several personal days I can use. Heaven knows I have worked at the airport long enough to prove myself a valued employee. Besides, I've hardly taken any days off since I got the job almost a year and a half ago. I'll tell my boss that I knew someone on the plane and his family in Houston needs me. That's partially true. I wouldn't be able to leave right away—which reminds me, I think my phone has lost its charge and I'd better check my messages. I'm sure there must be one from my boss telling me to be at the airport early tomorrow morning. Sunday is usually my day off, but with this situation, I'll need to be there. If they suspect a plane has crashed, they usually bring in a team of experts in public relations and grief counselors to handle the fallout of a tragedy like this. But they probably won't arrive until Monday. I think I could leave after that if my boss feels like everything is under control."

"Okay," he said, relief flooding over him. "I wonder if Paul has heard about the missing plane? Maybe we can send him a text message from your cell phone to tell him the meeting is still on, but that you will be taking my place. Set it up for Tuesday evening. Do you think that would work?"

She nodded. "I could leave either Monday or Tuesday morning at the latest. You know, in this age of 24-hour news, Johnson probably has heard about the plane already."

Jack yawned, and Lauren was suddenly aware that he must be

physically and mentally exhausted. They were both too tired to make any more rational decisions, and they knew the next several days would be long and taxing. Maybe after a good night's rest she might wake up from this strange dream. Had she really just offered to fly to Houston to help Jack?

"Let's talk more about this tomorrow," she said, finishing her glass of wine. She noticed that he'd finished his as well. "We can think more clearly in the morning after a good night's rest. You can sleep in the spare bedroom. Follow me." Jack grabbed his duffel bag and followed Lauren down the hall to the room she always kept ready for her sister.

When they entered, Lauren could see Jack was impressed. It was furnished with a double bed, rustic log bedposts, and a bedspread decorated with evergreen trees and brown moose silhouettes. A nightstand sat next to the bed with a lamp and a clock on it. The dark green lampshade gave off muted soft light, and with the hardwood floors and white wool woven rug, the room looked warm and comfortable. The walls held framed photos of Lauren's parents and her sister, Shannon, and Shannon's family.

Jack set down his bag and moved toward Lauren to give her a hug. This was too close for comfort, and she thought she'd better nip any physical contact ideas he had in the bud. She gently pushed him away. "Understand, Jack, that I'm no longer the naïve girl you dated in college. I'm not and never will be one of your tarts." That word came out without her having a chance to think about how ridiculous it sounded.

"Tarts? What's a tart? Isn't that a pastry?" He laughed.

"I just mean that, well, you have a reputation."

"That has been blown out of proportion to the extreme. For some reason, I'm a favorite target for the gossip mill, and I don't know why. Really, I go to a business lunch with a woman and the next thing I know, I'm hearing through the grapevine that I'm having an affair. It's ridiculous, and, of course, not true."

"What about the affairs you've had with married women?"

"What? Where do you hear this stuff? I have never dated a married woman and never will."

"Well, just rumors. People do talk. Remember Michelle Carter? She lives in Houston and loves to call and tell me what she's heard about you. Jealousy, I suppose. I think she had a thing for you. I understand you're both members of the same country club. She's probably still mad that you were a better skier than she was. You're probably a better golfer, too."

"I see her at the club occasionally. So that's where you're getting all this covert ridiculous information. God knows Michelle doesn't have anything else to do with her time but gossip about me. You know she married an oil executive and has everything she could want. She's bored. And yes, I am a better golfer than either of them."

"It's not all her. Your company does sometimes make the newspapers. It's not always good press."

He looked at her with intent blue eyes. "I'm glad I'm not me," he said.

Lauren was a bit taken aback. It wasn't like her to make accusations, and she felt a little embarrassed that she listened to rumors.

"You have to admit that you've left plenty of broken hearts in your wake," she said.

"Yes, most of them mine, I assure you."

"Why haven't you settled down?"

"Career mostly. A dangerous career that I didn't want to subject a family to. Also, it takes a lot of time and energy to get into this much trouble. And I've never found the right woman. It seems I only meet women who are interested in money and what it buys. I guess I won't have that problem after this is all over."

"I don't believe you could have gotten the reputation you have by being a monk, Jack."

"What about you, Mother Teresa?" he asked, turning the tables on Lauren. "You live here in Glitterville and you're a gorgeous woman. I'm sure you've had your share of lovers. You're sitting on a gold mine of a house, probably worth millions, in a city that's a playground for rich and powerful men who come from all over the world. I would have asked you to wait for me when I went to Harvard if I'd thought there was any chance . . ."

Jack stopped and looked at Lauren as if he'd said too much for a guy who always plays his cards close to his vest. Lauren momentarily felt embarrassed, although her heart started beating faster. Maybe he did still care about her.

"I guess I haven't found the right guy either," she said as she blushed and thought, *I would have waited for you, Jack, if you had asked. But that was then. This is now. You're desperate and you need my help. You'll say anything you think I want to hear. Can I trust you?*

"I'm sorry," she said gently. "I have no right to judge you." Turning to leave, she said, "I'm sure you remember the bathroom is down the hall. Make yourself at home and get a good night's sleep. Don't worry. These things have a way of working out. Good night, Jack."

Although she quickly turned away, she felt her face and her body grow warm with the thought of what his lips would feel like pressed against hers. She tried to suppress memories of long ago when she knew very well what his kisses felt like, and more. She continued down the hall to her bedroom, closed the door, and crawled into bed.

Jack sat on the guest bed, exhausted but exhilarated with the realization that he was very lucky to be alive.

CHAPTER 5

Early the next morning Lauren awoke with a start. Still pitch dark at five o'clock, she heard some clattering in the kitchen and realized Jack must be up. She found him making coffee.

"Good morning," she said as she entered the kitchen and took two coffee mugs out of the cupboard.

"Good morning. Did you sleep well?" he asked, his eyes on the glass coffee pot of water he was pouring into the coffee maker.

"Very well, thanks. How about you?"

"I slept like a rock, thanks to you and your hospitality. I hope you don't mind that I got up so early but I knew you would need to get to work and I wanted to talk to you first." He put the measured coffee grounds into the coffee maker and turned it on to start brewing. Leaning against the counter and facing her, he folded his arms.

Wearing only his jeans with no socks or shirt, Lauren found herself thinking how appealing he looked. She glanced away before he could read her mind.

"All my clothes need washing. Since I thought I was going home yesterday, that chore didn't get done," Jack said, offering an explanation for his state of dress. "Do you mind if I start a load of laundry?"

"Not at all. Laundry room's down the hall on the right."

At that affirmation, Jack unzipped his jeans and took them off right in front of her, then grabbed a small pile of clothes. Smiling at Lauren, wearing nothing but his briefs, he said, "I hope you don't mind seeing a little skin. I travel ski-bum light." Winking, he added, "And anyway, it's not anything you haven't seen before."

Lauren, feeling slightly embarrassed remembering their past sexual encounters, watched as he whisked his clothes into the small room that housed the washer and dryer. Contrary to Jack's offhand remark, she was not used to seeing half-naked men in her house. A warm surge coursed through her veins. Jack was in the same great shape that he'd been in twelve years ago, and she knew she couldn't concentrate on the business at hand with him looking as wonderful as he did.

"I have a spare robe. The house is a little cool," she said when Jack returned from the laundry room and she poured the two cups of coffee. She had previously purchased a plush white terry robe from a hotel to keep on hand when Shannon came to visit.

"That would be great, thanks."

Coming out of the guest bedroom, she handed it to him. It fit adequately but seemed snug across his chest.

"Why don't we turn on the news and see if they're reporting anything about the plane," Lauren suggested as they sipped their coffee. "Let's pray that it made a safe emergency landing somewhere and all the passengers are safe and unharmed."

Jack did not look optimistic as they walked into the living room and turned on the television. As expected, the missing plane was the top story on all the Denver morning news channels.

"An air search is underway to locate and investigate what authorities now believe is a downed private charter plane that lost contact with air traffic controllers outside Aspen yesterday." The newscaster then listed the six people believed to have been onboard, including Jack, an executive from Hewlett Packard, a Denver local news anchor and her

husband, along with the two pilots.

Lauren said, "A Denver local news anchor! That explains why the story made the news so soon yesterday. One of their own was on the plane."

"What do you mean?"

"Usually a plane that has lost contact, which happens often here, doesn't make the news for at least five hours. I was wondering about that."

Jack and Lauren gave each other knowing looks. Yesterday the gravity of the situation had been overwhelming, but today Lauren knew they could handle it. She wished circumstances had been different and she and Jack could focus on reminiscing and maybe on rekindling their relationship.

Jack said, "I guess we'd better get busy and work on our plan of action before you have to go to work. Do you have a laptop or a tablet?"

"I have both."

"Why don't we use the laptop?"

Clearly, Jack wanted to make sure Lauren was still comfortable with what she'd agreed to last night when he said, "Are you sure you'll be okay meeting with Paul Johnson, the witness I was supposed to meet? He said he has valuable information about the case, but wouldn't discuss it with me over the phone or email since we both came to the conclusion that my email had been hacked and someone was listening in on my phone conversations. He doesn't even live in Houston and was only staying there so that he could meet with me. Again, you could be in potential danger, as there is the possibility this may be why the plane is missing."

"Yes, I'm still willing to fly there and meet with him." Once Lauren set her mind to something, it was difficult to change it. Despite her misgivings, she was committed to helping Jack in any way possible. Through the years she'd had several boyfriends, but none of them could hold a candle to the way she felt when she'd been with Jack. Her heart told her that she had no choice. She had to help him, wherever it might lead her.

After thinking for a few minutes, Jack suggested, "First, why don't I transfer money into your bank account from a joint account I have with my dad to cover your travel expenses. I don't want to use my credit or debit card in case someone is watching for activity on it."

"Okay, that sounds like a good idea," Lauren responded, wondering if Jack was being paranoid or if they truly were involved in a strange and complicated conspiracy. She watched as Jack called up the bank accounts, asked for her information, and completed the transaction, all in the space of about five minutes.

"Now, could you go ahead and book a flight to Houston and a room at the Hyatt?"

"I should probably wait until I find out when I can leave," Lauren responded. "I have connections with the airlines, so I won't have any trouble finding a flight from Denver to Houston at the last minute. It might be hard to hitch a ride on a charter flight from here to Denver, but I think I can manage it."

"Using your feminine wiles?"

Lauren ignored the question. "I can also book the room later. Where did you want me to stay? Did you say the Hyatt?"

Jack nodded. "It's a great hotel. You should definitely stay there. We use it all the time for business associates."

"Sure, if you recommend it."

Lauren then sent the text to Paul Johnson from her phone. She asked if he'd heard about the missing plane and explained that she was a good friend of his and while in Aspen, Jack had asked her to contact him if anything were to happen to him. Would he be willing to meet with her in lieu of Jack?

Waiting for a response, Lauren moved to the kitchen and made a light breakfast. While eating, they shared friendly conversation, reminiscing about the past and what they had been doing in the years since college. It wasn't long before they heard the ring tone that indicated Paul had sent a text back. In his message, he said that he did hear about the plane and was devastated to think that something may have happened to Jack. He would be willing to meet with her if she came to Houston. Lauren then wrote back that she was planning on being in Houston Tuesday evening and would text him later about where to meet.

"Well, that's arranged," Lauren said with a hint of accomplishment in her voice.

"That's a load off of my shoulders. He has files he wanted to turn over to me. They're important. I don't think he would give them to you unless you met with him personally."

"I need to get dressed and get to work, Jack. My boss, David Richards, left me a message on my cell phone last night to come in as soon as possible this morning. It will be a busy morning. David will handle interviews with the media, they're always fascinated by air disasters. I'll be communicating with the family and business associates of the passengers that were onboard the plane, coordinating lodging and food for all of them, if and when they arrive in Aspen to await official word on the status of the plane. It won't be a fun day, and one that all of us in the airline industry dread."

"Does this happen often here?"

"Not often, but with Aspen's location and sometimes inclement weather, it does happen more frequently than at most other airports its size."

"I'm sorry that you have to do this. It must be a tough job."

"It comes with the territory," Lauren said, but she knew the look on her face, one of dread and worry, told a different story.

Lauren then went into her bedroom to dress and get ready for work. When she came out Jack had finished his laundry and was also dressed.

"What are you doing for lunch?" he asked.

"What's lunch?"

He laughed. "It's a meal humans partake in between the few specs of food that you ate this morning and the evening meal."

"I don't think my boss is aware of this ritual that you call lunch," Lauren teased. "Sorry, Jack, I won't be able to take time for lunch."

"The least I can do is have a dinner ready for you tonight, then. I'll go to the store. May I use your jeep?"

"Sure. Give me a ride to the airport, then you can use it all day."

Removing her keys from her purse, she set them on the coffee table.

"I'll disguise myself with a baseball cap and a spare pair of glasses I have with me," Jack said. "Normally, I wear contacts. I look much different with glasses. I haven't shaved, and my hair doesn't look anything like the picture they're flashing periodically on the television screen."

"I don't think anyone will recognize you," Lauren agreed. "This is a tourist town, so most customers are tourists. Shopkeepers don't make an effort to recognize them. We're all used to seeing famous people, so we try not to stare at anyone. Anyway, they have no reason to be looking for you. Give me your cell phone number so I can keep you posted if I find out anything about the plane, and I'll call you after I talk to my boss about leaving."

"Okay," Jack said as they both took out their phones. "I'll call you and you can capture my number."

As Jack tried to call Lauren he frowned. "My phone is dead," he said, going pale. "This is a company phone. Someone must have already had it disconnected. I guess they knew I wouldn't be coming back to work."

"Maybe you just forgot to charge it," Lauren offered.

"No, that's not it. I charged it last night."

Lauren shivered. She looked at Jack in disbelief, then composed herself long enough to say, "I have a landline here. I'll call you on that."

"I guess I'll have to get a burn phone while I'm out shopping for groceries."

"Are they expensive? Take my credit card if you need it." She took her credit card from her purse and gave it to Jack.

"Thanks. I'll never be able to thank you enough for all you're doing for me."

As she walked to the door to leave for work, her landline phone rang.

"That is probably Shannon. I knew she would call. I'm surprised she didn't call last night when she first heard about the missing plane. How much should I tell her?"

"Whatever you think is best, but I wouldn't tell her about me."

"I don't think I can lie to her. We don't keep secrets from each other."

"I wouldn't want you to lie to her, but it might be best if, for right now, you don't tell her everything—about me. Not yet, anyway."

"Okay, I understand."

Lauren answered the phone. As predicted, it was Shannon. She'd heard about the missing plane.

"Hi, Shannon."

"I just saw on the news there's a plane missing that took off from your airport yesterday," Shannon blurted.

"I know. I saw it, too. That's why I'm on my way to the airport, even though it's my day off. My boss is expecting me."

"That's terrible!"

"Tell me about it. I'm still trying to take it all in."

"The news said that Jack Kelly was on the plane. Isn't that the guy you dated in college?"

"That's why I'm having such a hard time processing it. The whole thing is so tragic."

"I can't imagine what you're going through. I know that Jack held a special place in your heart. I always believed that was why you've never had a serious relationship since."

"Well, I don't think that's quite the reason." Lauren took a breath. Jack was standing nearby, listening.

"Did you see him when he was in Aspen?" Shannon asked.

"I did see him yesterday, just before the plane took off. That's why this is so hard on me."

"You did? Oh Lauren . . ."

"I'm sorry, but I can't talk right now. I'm in a rush to get to the airport. They need my help with public relations and travel arrangements for family members of the passengers."

"Oh, of course. You must be frantic."

"I'll call you again as soon as things quiet down, okay?"

"Sure. Take care of yourself, Lauren. And call if you need me."

Lauren hung up the phone and told Jack, "Shannon wouldn't tell anyone. But if you think it is best she doesn't know anything right now, I understand."

"I know that you don't like to keep things from your sister, but I think it would be best if she remains unaware of me and my predicament, and I thank you for not mentioning it."

"You're welcome. And now I have to leave. I'll take the shuttle home around six o'clock. Let me give you my cell number if you need me."

She wrote down her number on a pad of paper and then they headed out the door toward the airport.

CHAPTER 6

David Richards, administrator of the Aspen regional airport, prepared for the day ahead. This was the last thing he needed, he thought to himself in the very early hours of Sunday morning as he looked in the mirror and tied his tie. A plane has lost radio contact, and not just any plane, a plane carrying VIPs. Among the passengers, a native of Colorado whose dad was a well-known college football coach, an executive from a major well-known company and—he just found out—an admired local Denver news anchor and her husband, a Saudi national and former ambassador to the United States. You could not have made up a list that would create a more sensational media frenzy.

The airport had been incredibly busy and challenging this year, and now a missing plane cast a spotlight on him and Aspen. He longed for the quiet, laid-back life he'd had before coming to the United States. An expert skier and one-time Olympic hopeful originally from Calgary, Alberta, Canada, David moved to Colorado to marry a woman he'd met during one of his trips to Aspen for a winter athletic competition. That was years ago—now his kids were teenagers. His wife, Mary, kept occupied with her own hobbies and interests while he worked long hours to keep the airport running efficiently during ski season, dealing with challenges above and beyond the normal personnel problems and many difficult situations that came up during a busy week. Ironically, he had little time to ski, which was what had brought him to Colorado in the first place.

Wondering if he should kiss his sleeping wife goodbye before leaving, he decided against waking her up. *Why bother her this early? She'll see me on the news shortly, anyway.* He poured himself coffee into a commuter mug with the intention of eating a quick breakfast at the airport. Taking his keys from the key holder by the door, he headed out to face a grueling and long day.

Lauren hit the ground running as soon as she arrived at the airport. Phones were ringing and people bustled about, performing their many duties. Her boss was already meeting with reporters, and a news conference had been set up for ten o'clock, initiated by him and the FAA. The plane had still not been heard from or located.

The Colorado chapter of the Civil Air Patrol was conducting an air search for the missing plane, using Aspen's airport as a base in conjunction with Eagle/Vail, and other front range airfields.

Lauren spent the day making travel arrangements and accommodations for family members who wanted to come and await word from the investigators. She also handled all of David's routine calls, since he was busy with the news media and another million things.

She stole a few minutes away from the mayhem to walk down to the maintenance office, where she found the manager, Carl, at his desk. Carl was one of her closest friends in Aspen. His office was lined with various certificates of accomplishments, proof that he was the best in his field. He had been working with the investigators, and she was lucky to find him taking a short break.

He smiled when he looked up and saw Lauren. "Hi. I see you're here on your day off, too," he said as he motioned for her to sit down in a chair by his desk.

"I guess we all have our work cut out for us. That's what happens with this kind of event."

Carl nodded.

"Any thoughts?" Lauren asked.

"It was a private charter plane, but we did check it out before take off. Everything looked fine and in good working order."

"Are there any theories floating around?"

"Anything could have happened. Pilot error is our always our first thought, but I wouldn't rule out mechanical problems. Things happen. It could also be sabotage, and I assume that's what others are thinking, judging by the passenger list and all the agencies that have shown up here today. Since the flight was a private charter, the security procedures aren't the same as they are with a commercial flight. It looks to me like someone on that plane might have had an enemy."

Lauren could feel the blood drain out of her face. Even though she feared the worst, to hear Carl suggest it shook her up.

"They're conducting an air search for the plane right now and have already begun an investigation. We should know something soon. Are you all right, Lauren? You look a little pale."

"Yes, I'm fine. To tell you the truth, I knew someone on the plane, and I am upset. I'm going to ask David if I can leave tomorrow to help attend to his family in Houston."

"Really? I'm so sorry. Who was it?"

"Jack Kelly. He was an old family friend."

"Geez. I'm surprised you can work at all. It's hard enough to comfort families of people you don't know. How have you been able to hold up?"

At that moment, members of the FAA stormed into Carl's office. They looked at Lauren as if they preferred a private conversation with Carl. She took the cue and excused herself before Carl had a chance to introduce her.

Lauren continued working nonstop throughout the day and did a tremendous job of juggling her many duties. By six o'clock she was exhausted but still needed to talk to her boss about leaving. She found the ex-pat Canadian in his office as she walked by. He looked frazzled and exhausted. His eyes looked red, almost like he had been crying, and she immediately became concerned for him. They talked briefly and then she carefully repeated to him what she had just revealed to Carl .

"Of course you should leave, get out of here," David said with gentle concern. "I didn't realize that you had a family friend on the plane. Jack Kelly—is that the guy from Colorado whose father was the football coach at CU?"

"One and the same. His dad now lives in Houston and isn't in very good health. Jack doesn't have any other family. So, I would like to go see him and help him through this."

"Sure, Lauren. We have reinforcements coming in tomorrow. They are already on their way. They'll help with the media, the investigation, and continue your work with the accommodations for people from out of town. I'm sure you have everything under control. Maybe you could come in for a few hours tomorrow morning to get the new team up to speed, but after that, feel free to leave so you can attend to your friend's family and deal with your own sadness and anxiety. We'll be fine."

David was a kind and caring man who always put his employees first. She was lucky to have a boss with a heart. That was one of the reasons she enjoyed her job, and, therefore, it was not easy for her to lie to him. Her voice sounded shaky when she talked, and her only consolation was that because she'd worked so hard during the day, things were now under control. So, the team that was scheduled to arrive the next day would have no problem taking over her duties. She wished David well and they said goodnight. Lauren wondered how much longer David would have to stay before he would be able to leave for the evening. What would his wife be thinking, or did she care at all? Lauren had heard through the grapevine that David's marriage was rocky. He and his wife had been drifting apart and she suspected from the rumors that there was infidelity on both sides.

Lauren left the airport and caught the shuttle to her house. As she approached her property, she could see that there were no lights on and her jeep was not out front as it should have been. She felt slightly sick as she realized Jack, with her credit card and her jeep, wasn't anywhere to be found. Where was he? As she slowly walked to her front door and slid the key into the lock, her jeep pulled up to the front of her house.

Jack got out of the vehicle holding a bouquet of roses. "I forgot the most important part of the evening," he said as he walked up to greet her. "I had the food ready and decided to run out and get you these. You must be very tired. I hope you like the dinner I prepared. If you can point me to a vase, I'll put these roses in water and we'll be set."

Lauren laughed at how different Jack looked wearing a baseball cap over disheveled hair and thick, dark-rimmed glasses that dramatically altered his appearance. He looked nothing like the handsome man in the picture being flashed on the news reports. She, herself, would have never recognized him. *No wonder he wears contacts. I didn't realize he was that near-sighted.*

"I guess you've never seen me with these glasses. I told you I looked different in them," Jack said as Lauren handed him a vase from the kitchen cabinet. He filled it with water and arranged the roses inside it.

"Believe me, you don't look the same at all. I guess I do remember you wore contacts in college." Lauren was pleased that he'd been so thoughtful to buy roses. "They're my favorite shade of pink. Thanks very much, Jack!" She told herself to cool it, not think anything romantic right now. She didn't fully trust him, and he knew her weak spots.

Jack replied, "You're welcome. I'm really not such a cad, in spite of what some people say."

Lauren chose to ignore that. "Am I right to assume no one recognized you? How was your day shopping?"

"I had a great day shopping. I forgot Aspen pedestrian protocol, though. I was standing at the curb and another guy next to me stepped off, into the street, and all the cars stopped."

"That's the way things are done here," Lauren smiled.

"Trust me, that is not the way it's done in Houston. If anything, drivers speed up to hit you. Keep that in mind."

Lauren laughed. "Okay, I will. I'll be careful crossing the streets there."

They entered her kitchen and walked toward a beautifully set table with candles lit and china place settings atop a linen tablecloth. He'd uncorked the wine and the presentation of a wonderful chicken Marsala meal was heavenly. She was famished.

Jack poured the wine, then pulled out Lauren's chair and said, "During my shopping trip today I bought a burn cell phone and used your credit card. I transferred money from my dad's bank account into yours. I'm a joint owner of his account. No one at Last Defense is aware of that account, so we're good. Now, let's eat!"

"Thank you, Jack. It looks fabulous."

The meal was delicious, and the evening hours slipped away as they caught up on both good and bad times since they'd left college. Amid frequent laughter and things they found they still had in common, Lauren was surprised how easily the two of them were able to talk. Jack had always made her laugh, and that hadn't changed. It seemed like the spark between them still remained, despite the passing of time. Then Lauren asked the question she'd wanted to ask Jack since she'd first seen him at the airport.

"Why didn't you keep in touch with me after you left for Harvard? You promised that you would. I'd hoped we would at least be friends, even though we lived in different states and I knew you would find someone else. Was I that easy to forget?"

"I did try to contact you," Jack said in a nonchalant tone of voice. "I called and left messages—since no one was ever home to answer the phone. I even sent you a letter, to this address, and it came back to me stamped *Unknown Address—Return to Sender.* I thought you had given up on me and moved on." He looked at her with sincerity in his eyes. "I heard through the grapevine that you were dating CU class president, Jim Prescott. I didn't think I should interfere. I figured that's why you weren't returning my calls."

"Now who listens to rumors?" Lauren said with a smile on her face. "I went out a couple times with Jim, but we were just friends, never serious. My parents rented out this place occasionally, and it doesn't surprise me that the tenants didn't give me your phone messages. But I still should have received your letter. That's really strange."

"I still have the letter. I can even show it to you."

"No, you're kidding. From over ten years ago?"

"I guess I'm more sentimental than you think. I looked at it occasionally when I had an urge to contact you just to remind me that you had moved on."

Lauren was taken aback by this revelation. If Jack was telling the truth, she had been under the wrong impression about him all these years. How foolish she'd been to listen to Michelle and not her own heart. She thought he had forgotten about her, never really loved her, and was busy living the single life, a player, with not even a vague memory of their relationship. But for her, those romantic feelings for him still ran deep. He was her first love.

Changing the subject, Lauren confided, "By the way, my boss said that I could leave for Houston tomorrow. He was very understanding." She relayed their conversation.

"That's great. Are you still willing to go?"

"Of course. In the morning, I'll make the final travel arrangements. I already found a commuter flight to Denver. I'll book a commercial flight from Denver to Houston and make the hotel reservation. It will be all set."

"Lauren, I wouldn't blame you if you have second thoughts and want to cancel. No harm—no foul."

"No, I don't have second thoughts. Why do you ask?"

"My phone being turned off unnerved me a little. I'm starting to have serious doubts about everyone at Last Defense."

"I'm just going there to meet with Paul. I won't get near Last Defense."

She then told Jack about her conversation with Carl. Jack didn't seem surprised. He suspected that the investigation would be focused on pilot error or sabotage. There'd been no weather related problems that night, and mechanical failure was unlikely.

After dinner, Jack and Lauren tried to watch a movie on television but Lauren couldn't keep her eyes open.

"Why don't you go ahead and go to bed? I'll clean up. You've had a long day."

"You're right. I'll never make it through the movie. Guess you'll have to tell me how it ends," Lauren said as she stood up and made her way to her bedroom.

Jack sat on the couch for a few moments after Lauren left and contemplated his decision to trust her. He had never realized before how capable she was. She must have had a stressful day consoling and helping anxious and upset family members. And then, always in the back of her mind would be lurking the possibility that the plane was missing because of the actions of someone at Last Defense and that person's relationship to the man hiding out at her house. Something she had knowledge of but couldn't tell anyone.

Jack appreciated Lauren's strength and resilience. She easily could have called the authorities by now and turned him in, then continued living her safe, comfortable life. He hoped that she trusted him as much as he trusted her. No doubt about it, Lauren was the best and brightest person he could ask for to go to Houston and meet with Paul on his behalf.

CHAPTER 7

Arising early to get a fresh start on another busy day, Lauren found Jack in the kitchen, again playing chef, this time preparing a full breakfast. Lauren stood looking on, impressed with his culinary skills.

"Where and when did you learn to cook like this?"

"I'm a man of many talents," he quipped as he handed her a plate of pancakes smothered with fresh strawberries, sprinkled with powdered sugar. Link sausages rounded out the meal, along with freshly squeezed orange juice and brewed coffee.

Preparing for her mission in Houston during breakfast, Lauren initiated a conversation about Jack's company. She wanted to be ready for any and all possibilities.

"Tell me more about Last Defense," she said as she took a bite of sausage.

"The private security contractor business sprung up to become a multi-billion-dollar industry within the last few years. I met Michael Dodson several years ago through friends at the country club I belong to. I had the best of intentions and so did he. The industry lacks oversight, and we were trying to change that through Michael's connections in Washington."

"What did you mean Saturday night when you said you had

lost contact with your conscience?"

"Sometimes you end up doing things that you don't feel totally comfortable about—mostly hiring locals to execute some of the most dangerous missions. A lot of Afghani men are desperate and will take on a job that puts them at risk because they need the money. It's hard to sleep nights when dealt a bad outcome, which is often the case."

"I see."

"We have been trying to diversify. We've been getting more involved in training and other types of security services."

"Who is Paul Johnson?"

"I'm not really sure. I believe he works for another contractor and was friends with Omar Kasim, our employee who was ambushed and killed in Afghanistan."

The sadness on Jack's face was unmistakable as he continued with his story.

"Paul contacted me a couple weeks ago and said he needed to talk to me. He said he had suspicions about what happened to Omar."

"And that didn't sit well with Michael?"

"No. We've been advised by our lawyers not to talk to anyone, but I have to hear what Paul has to say. Omar was a friend, and I can't play this corporate game anymore."

"So you knew Omar well?"

"Yes. Omar's dad, Ali Kasim, and my dad knew each other from the country club. They were both military veterans and had a lot in common. That's how I got to know Omar, and how, subsequently, he came to work for Last Defense. When my dad started losing his memory and it became obvious he couldn't live on his own anymore, Ali and Omar were very supportive."

"Your dad must have been older than your mom, if I remember right."

"Yes, my mom was his second wife. He was about twenty years older. He never recovered from losing her to cancer about five years ago. That was another reason the Kasim's friendship was so important to him."

"Where would we be without friends and family to look out for us, eh?"

"That reminds me, how is your cousin Eric doing, other than he's landed a great job?"

"He's doing good. He has a girlfriend and I think it's serious. I haven't met her yet, but I understand she's charming."

"I'm glad to hear that."

"Your father really helped him. He was getting ready to drop out of college when your dad intervened and put him on the right path."

"Do you think Eric was on drugs?"

Lauren shook her head. "No, I don't think he was using. I think he just needed to belong to a group. The group he ended up with was a bunch of losers. But then, with your father's help he became part of the football team and he totally turned around. It was a remarkable change."

After breakfast, Lauren got out her laptop and made the necessary travel and hotel arrangements for her trip to Houston.

Taking out her cell phone, she said to Jack, "Call me so that I can capture your new burn cell phone number."

Jack followed her instructions, calling her from his new phone.

"Got it. You obviously have my cell phone number, so we're good to go. Now, where should I meet Paul?" Lauren asked, ready to send a text.

"Why don't you just meet him at the bar in the lobby of the Hyatt? That would be convenient, then you won't have to leave the hotel. It's a public place, so that should make both of you feel comfortable. How about five o'clock tomorrow evening? The bar will be crowded, but not too crowded at that time."

"Sounds good."

She sent another text to Paul and went to her bedroom to get ready for work and her trip. She traveled often, so her suitcase always contained a few essential items. For two nights in Houston a few outfits should be all she needed. She was ready to go on her adventure and a little glad to be leaving. The anticipation of the trip was nerve-racking, but she didn't want to be alone again with Jack for another night, afraid she might succumb to her physical attraction to him and his raw masculinity. The danger of their situation had ignited strong emotions. Whatever danger awaited her in Houston didn't seem as threatening as spending another night in the same house with this handsome man and former lover.

Jack gave her a ride to the airport in her jeep. As they neared the terminal, she found herself starting to feel some doubts about whether or not she should place herself in such a risky situation. But at this point, it was too late, for second thoughts. At curbside, Jack leaned over and hugged her. As she turned to leave, he grabbed her arm and drew her toward him, kissing her passionately on the lips, unafraid that she would again rebuff him. Instead, she looked into his eyes, hoping to see a sincerity and a longing that she had feared was gone. She thought she had her answer, but how could she tell for sure? She pulled herself away. "I'll keep in touch regularly by phone," she reassured him, but she could tell that he was apprehensive.

"Lauren, do you want to call the mission off?" he asked again, but she wouldn't budge. She was only going to meet with a witness. What could go wrong?

She got out of the car, waved goodbye to Jack and quickly walked into the airport. After filling in the employees that would take her place, she prepared for her own trip. By noon, she was on a plane to Denver with a connecting flight to Houston.

CHAPTER 8

Lauren's flight from Aspen to Denver International Airport on Monday afternoon was short, allowing her little time to relax. She looked down at the beautiful snow-covered mountains that seemed to stretch on and on. It was more pleasant to focus on the view rather than on the mission she had committed to. She couldn't help but wonder where the lost plane was.

Paul Johnson had replied to her text message, agreeing to the time and place for their meeting. Everything was falling into place.

The layover in Denver provided just enough time for her to grab a snack before catching the connecting flight to Houston. After buckling into her seat, she leaned back and closed her eyes. As the plane taxied for takeoff, the thoughts she'd tried to suppress during the brief shuttle flight returned.

Why am I leaving my warm, cozy house for a man I haven't seen in over twelve years?

Her sense of adventure and wanting to help was part of it. Also, she felt she owed Jack's father for helping her cousin. Then there was the most important reason of all—she realized that she still had deep feelings for Jack and couldn't sit by while someone was trying to kill him, if that was truly the situation.

Was it true that over the years he had tried to keep in touch with her, or had he just said that to make sure she would help him? The proof would be the unopened letter. She wanted to see it. Maybe they could rekindle their relationship. If so, she wouldn't be alone anymore. Was Jack the one?

She had felt alone since losing her parents. She was close to her sister, but Shannon had everything she wanted—she was happily married to her high school sweetheart, and they had two adorable children. Shannon's husband had been there to support her, but Lauren hadn't had anyone to talk to. Lauren still felt lonely even though it had been over a year since her parents' tragic accident. Would she ever enter a serious relationship?

When she'd found out that her parents had left their house to both sisters, Lauren knew that Shannon didn't want to uproot her family and move to Aspen. That's when she decided to take a chance and leave Denver, knowing she'd miss her friends and her sister, but since she was alone and had never ventured off by herself, she felt that the time was right to make the change. And the job at the Aspen airport had miraculously opened up shortly after she moved, so everything had worked out well.

About halfway into the approximately two-hour flight, Lauren tried to read the magazines she'd bought in Denver. The flight attendant asked if she wanted anything to drink, she requested a diet soda and enjoyed the nuts that came with it.

As she gazed out the window of the plane, memories crept back into her mind. Memories of one of the times Jack had been in her Aspen house, many years ago. Her parents were out of town, and it was one of the few times they had gotten to be alone for an entire evening.

Even though she had tried to forget through the years, she remembered that night. She had done little more than kiss a man before that evening. Jack was her first sexual encounter, and she would never forget it.

What made sex with Jack Kelly so incredible? He was tender but at the same time rough and demanding. He was also playful, which she missed in the few sexual encounters she'd had since Jack.

What a night! Lauren had made dinner and they had almost finished a bottle of wine. Handing another glass to him, she boldly said, "Why don't we move to the bedroom? My parents are out of town and won't be home tonight."

"Sounds like a good idea to me," he responded. He wore a T-shirt and blue jeans and looked so sexy. They both sat down on the bed, and when Jack settled next to Lauren, she cuddled up next to him. The cozy fire they had made in the hearth earlier in the evening had long ago expired, and the house was cooling down. All Lauren could think about was the heat generated by him sitting next to her, and how comfortable she felt. "I feel your warmth, and I can feel your heartbeat," she said. "You feel great. How do you taste?"

"Let's find out."

Jack slipped his arm around her and kissed her deeply. She couldn't resist his strong embrace and the passion she was feeling toward him. She kissed back, and he responded with his tongue. What bliss she was feeling as she folded her arms around his neck and he reached behind her back to unfasten her bra, then he tenderly caressed her breasts.

"Don't think you can take advantage of me because we're alone, without our usual chaperones," she said teasingly since she had initiated the encounter.

"I would never take advantage of you. I've wanted you for such a long time."

"I've wanted you, too."

She reached down to unbutton and unzip his jeans. Both his shirt and jeans came off faster than she could catch her breath.

When he pressed his body against hers, forcing her to lie back with him on top, she willingly surrendered to her desire for him.

Lauren jumped, startled from her erotic memories by the

overhead speaker announcing the plane's descent into Houston Intercontinental Airport. After a smooth landing and the long walk to the baggage area, she was feeling energized again. By the time she picked up her suitcase from the carousel, it was late afternoon.

Since she had never been to Houston before and was unfamiliar with the city, she took a taxi instead of renting a car. It was raining hard, and she was glad she'd had the foresight to bring her khaki raincoat and umbrella.

First on her agenda was a trip to see Jack's dad, Rick Kelly. This was a personal mission and couldn't wait another day. She wanted to see him, thinking that somehow it might bring her closer to Jack.

CHAPTER 9

The private facility specializing in dementia and Alzheimer's care that Jack had arranged for his dad seemed clean and pleasant. Lauren knew that he would find the best for Rick but this place exceeded her expectations. It was a comfortable converted house with ten residents.

"You have a visitor," the aide said as she directed Lauren into Rick's room. It had a large private bath, an outdoor patio, and was beautifully decorated. Lauren felt a deep personal satisfaction that Rick was getting the very best care possible. The aides and other personnel seemed kind and professional.

Rick was sitting up in a comfortable recliner. Lauren sat down across from him took his hands into her own, and with a smile quietly said, "Hello." She spoke to him in a loving, gentle tone, telling him who she was and her relationship to him and Jack. She could see his familiar face light up to find a friendly visitor but saw no sign of recognition whatsoever. It didn't take a medical degree to know that Rick was suffering from an advanced form of dementia, whether it was Alzheimer's or simply memory loss caused by something else, it broke her heart to see him like that.

Glancing around the room, Lauren noticed a rain jacket slung over one of the other chairs. Then she suddenly realized a man had entered the room. She quickly got up and held out her hand.

"Hi. I'm Lauren Reese. I'm a friend from Colorado."

The stranger shook her hand. "Michael Dodson."

Lauren tried to conceal the shock and apprehension she felt at the sound of the name she'd just heard. Why on earth was Jack's business partner here in his dad's room? Instinctively, she stepped back and gathered her composure, trying to act like she had never heard his name before.

If he noticed her surprise, he hid it well.

"You're from Colorado?" he continued. "I was in the hallway returning from the kitchen, and overheard what you told Rick. I've been here awhile and was just getting ready to leave. May I have a word with you in private, please?"

"Sure, of course." Lauren leaned over to Rick. "I'll be right back," she told him gently.

Michael said his goodbyes to Rick and picked up his rain jacket. Lauren followed him through the hallway, past the dining area, and into the open room where visitors typically waited. The room was furnished with a comfortable couch and several large plush chairs, none of which were occupied. Michael sat down on the couch with his rain jacket in his lap, and Lauren took a seat next to him. A ruggedly handsome man, thirtyish, blonde hair and brown eyes, Michael Dodson had a slight British accent and seemed very self-assured. He was not at all what she'd expected.

"I wanted to talk to you privately," he said, gazing at her intently. "Are you here because of the lost plane in Aspen?"

Lauren nodded, knowing she had to come up with an impromptu story. "I was a friend of Jack's, and he had asked me to look after his affairs if anything ever happened to him."

"First, if my assumption is true, let me say that I was incredibly sorry to hear about Jack. Since they haven't located the plane we can only assume the worst. He was one of the best men I've ever known, as well as a good friend. I'm really going to miss him." Michael sounded as if he meant it. "Were the two of you close?"

"We were college sweethearts and had kept in touch through the years. I also know Rick very well. He was the coach at CU when I was a student there and became a close family friend."

"I am, or should I say was, Jack's business partner. I'm very pleased to meet you. I was wondering if there is anything I could do to help Rick. And as for you, I'm glad that Jack had the foresight to make arrangements in case anything happened to him."

Lauren was taken aback. *Why would he think that? Unless he knew that Jack had a reason to be worried something would happen. Was Michael the one responsible for the missing plane?*

"Do you have power of attorney?" Michael asked, looking genuinely concerned. "Are you the administrator of his estate? Have you contacted his lawyer yet? There is so much to do."

"I just got off the plane, so I haven't had a chance to do too much yet. I work at the airport in Aspen, so it was difficult for me to get away. As you can imagine, I've been very busy. And yes, I do have power of attorney." This last part was a fabrication, but she had to appear legitimate.

"Another reason I wanted to talk to you alone is that I don't think we should mention anything to Rick about the plane right now. I don't know if he even knows who Jack is anymore. Sometimes he does and sometimes he doesn't. I'm sure there is a provision in Jack's will to take care of him. He was a caring son and was responsible to a fault. There is a degree of danger with the business we are in, and it requires us to think ahead and make plans for our loved ones—just in case, as I'm sure Jack had told you."

"Yes, he told me about the business." Lauren found herself admitting respect for Michael and his insight and kindness in not wanting to upset Rick. She also felt warmly toward Jack, knowing that obviously he was capable of caring for someone very much. "I agree there is no reason to tell Rick anything about the plane at this time. I'll assume responsibility for taking care of him and I'll find out all the arrangements that Jack made."

"That's great," Michael said as he looked at her with relief showing on his face—and something more—a look of interest. Lauren allowed herself a guarded smile.

"One less thing to worry about," Michael said as he stood up to leave. "Well, I'll let you continue your visit with Rick. It's very nice to meet you, Lauren. We should stay in touch. I'd like to see you again. Would you like to stop by the office tomorrow?"

"Sure," she said apprehensively, remembering she had promised Jack she wouldn't go near the Last Defense office.

"Just let me know when." He reached in his pocket and pulled out his wallet, "Here's my business card. Where are you staying?"

"I have a room at the Hyatt."

"Good choice. That's where our clients stay when they're in town. We have connections there. I'll make sure you're getting the best room available." He smiled and nodded to her slightly, and left.

Lauren was a bit shaken at running into Michael so quickly. She thought for a few moments about the encounter. Michael didn't meet her expectations of someone cold and calculating. He didn't seem like a cold-blooded killer, either. A murderer wouldn't be kind enough to visit an elderly gentleman and be concerned about his welfare. She was starting to think that Jack was being paranoid, his imagination getting the best of him. Jack did confide in her that he was under a lot of stress.

Feeling confident that she couldn't possibly be in danger, and thinking that Jack's relationship with Michael was a misunderstanding and nothing more, she got up from the couch and returned to Rick's room. He was watching a football game on television and seemed to be able to follow the plays. Conversation was limited because of Rick's condition, but he seemed happy to see her again so she held his hand and they watched the game together in silence.

CHAPTER 10

Lauren spent over an hour with Rick watching the football game, then said goodbye and called a taxi. She was tired, and anxious to check into her hotel room at the Hyatt Regency. Dusk had fallen. The rain had stopped and humidity saturated the air, so different from the fresh, crisp mountain air in Aspen.

The ride to the hotel proved uneventful. Few cars traveled the road on this rainy Monday night. Lauren closed her eyes to the bright lights that reflected off the wet streets and buildings as they wound their way through town.

As Lauren checked into the Hyatt, she got another surprise.

"We've received a phone call from Mr. Michael Dodson, miss. You're room has been upgraded to a luxury suite on the sixth floor. Last Defense will be picking up the charges." the hotel clerk told her.

Dumfounded by the generous gesture, Lauren thanked the clerk, took the card key, then made her way to the elevator and onto the sixth floor. She didn't know whether to be flattered or afraid of this new development.

She found the suite to be exceptional and well appointed. The foyer featured a desk and chair, a coat rack, and an umbrella stand, complete with umbrella. A large mirror hung on the wall above the desk. There was a flat screen TV in the front room, as well as a couch and loveseat. Walking down a short hallway, she passed a little kitchenette area on the left and a bathroom on the right which led to the bedroom that featured a big closet, a king size bed and end tables with decorative lamps on each one.

After unpacking her suitcase and resting for a few moments, she sat down on the bed and used her cell phone to call Jack to let him know she'd arrived safely in Houston and had visited his dad. She told him that Rick seemed happy and was being well cared for. Casually, she mentioned that she had already met Michael, but, afraid of his reaction, didn't tell him that he had upgraded her hotel room and that the company was picking up the charges.

Lauren could tell that Jack seemed pleased that she had stopped in to see his dad. But when she mentioned her encounter with Michael, he sounded unnerved and anxious.

"You've got to be kidding. What are the odds that he would be there when you stopped by? Please be careful," he said with deep concern in his voice. "He may seem charming, but you need to be incredibly suspicious of him and his motives. Stick to the plan. You're only there to meet with Paul Johnson, and afterward you're to come right home."

"Don't worry. I will. Hopefully, Paul will give us some answers. I'm very interested in what he has to say." She didn't see how she could be in danger. Michael seemed like a perfect gentleman, and she was starting to be convinced that the two of them were just having differences and the typical arguments that business partners often have, similar to a married couple going through a divorce. Hopefully, the plane would be located soon and the investigation would clear everyone of any sabotage activity. She would spend the next day relaxing at the hotel, meet Paul, and then fly home. After that, and what might happen with Jack, she had no clue.

"Just be very careful. Trust no one." And then Jack blurted, "I wish I could be there with you."

"Really, I don't feel like I'm in any danger," she said as she tried to convince him. And then, unsure how to handle his last comment, she simply said, "Goodnight."

"I didn't think I was in danger, either, Lauren. All I'm saying is watch your back."

Next, Lauren called Shannon. She couldn't lie to her sister anymore and felt she had to update her on the situation and where she was. Shannon always seemed to have a level head on her shoulders and was full of advice, although Shannon's advice wasn't always what Lauren wanted to hear.

"Shannon, are you busy? We need to talk."

"I'm glad you called. I've been anxious to hear from you. I knew you'd call as soon as you had a chance, but I was starting to get concerned."

"I have a lot to tell you. Jack wasn't on the plane—the one that lost contact with ground control. Please don't tell anyone. It's a long story. I've talked to him, and he thinks the plane may have been sabotaged. For that reason he doesn't want anyone to know quite yet that he wasn't on it."

"Are you serious? Is this true?"

"It is hard to believe, but it's true."

"You've talked to him?"

"Yes, he came to see me after he heard about the plane."

"Why would he think the plane was sabotaged? Where is he?'

"He's at our house in Aspen. We're trying to sort things out. I'm in Houston at the Hyatt Regency Hotel. I left Aspen today. I wasn't going to tell you because I didn't want you to worry, but I can't keep secrets from you."

"Why Houston, Lauren?"

"This is where Jack lives, and this is where his business is."

"Are you in any danger? This doesn't sound good to me."

"No, I'm safe, but thanks for asking. Please don't worry."

"Why are you even involved?"

She told her sister why she'd decided to travel to Houston. Then she filled her in on the details.

"I'm planning to meet with the man that Jack was scheduled to meet with. He'll hand over some files he has, and hopefully, the information in them will help Jack. They must be important."

"I wouldn't be a very good big sister if I wasn't concerned," Shannon concluded.

Lauren downplayed her sister's concerns. "I'm going to be playing messenger, that's all. No big deal. I'll be back home Wednesday."

"Well," Shannon said, "you've always had a sense of curiosity and adventure, so I'm not too surprised that you took on this project. And I know how you've felt about Jack, even though you've tried to hide your feelings through the years. Are you confident that you know what you are doing?"

"Yes, I am. I'm starting to think that Jack's imagination is taking over his life. He is under a lot of stress and he's very overworked. I've already met his business partner, and the man seems like a nice guy. All this is probably just a strange and tragic coincidence. If it turns out the plane was sabotaged, there were other passengers aboard and therefore other suspects."

"Please be extra careful. I don't want to lose my sister and my best friend. Always make sure you've got an escape plan for any situation. Do you have protection, like pepper spray or something?"

"Thanks for the good advice. Don't worry. I can take care of myself. That's a good idea about the pepper spray. I'll pick some up tomorrow. Really, I'll be fine. I'll call you again and let you know what I find out after I talk to this witness tomorrow night."

With that, Lauren ended the phone call, and felt her stomach grumble. She'd forgotten to eat supper during her busy evening.

Not feeling like venturing out again for food, she called room service and ordered a sandwich. Watching a good movie while she ate kept her from worrying about tomorrow.

When the movie ended, she glanced at her watch. It read ten o'clock, but it was eleven o'clock Houston time. After resetting it, she walked down the hall to the bedroom. Thoroughly exhausted, she snuggled down into the warm covers of the king-size bed and fell asleep immediately.

CHAPTER 11

Noises from the hallway outside the room awoke Lauren from a pleasant dream of skiing with Jack. The dream brought back wonderful memories of their many trips together. Normally, Jack liked to take on the Bell Mountain runs, but those were too challenging for Lauren. Instead, he would ski the slopes that were in her comfort level just so that they could steal kisses on the chairlift, much to the chagrin of the other two people on the lift. Seeing Jack again must have brought back this special memory but she couldn't linger over it. She had to get up and face the day.

It was Tuesday. She would meet with Paul Johnson at 5 o'clock, find out his story, and take possession of the files he wanted to turn over to Jack. Then, she would go back to her comfortable mountain home and life in Aspen. Maybe rekindle her relationship with Jack, or at least get to know him again. Getting out of bed, she put on the plush hotel bathrobe and walked to the shower. Stepping inside, she let jets of warm water fall upon her shoulders and felt energized to meet the day.

Her thoughts drifted to the men with whom she'd recently come in contact. She felt like life had changed significantly this week. First there was Jack, who had interrupted her routine with his potentially dangerous and uncertain situation. Along with Jack came the bittersweet memories of first love, which left her to wonder what to make of her mixed feelings about him. Then there was Jack's dad, Rick, to whom she hoped she'd offered some small comfort. Michael Dodson, an enigma, the man in charge of Last Defense who probably had more secrets to hide than anyone else she'd ever met, had captivated her with his charm. Part of her wished she'd had the opportunity to talk with Michael longer, but she guessed that wasn't meant to be. The next scheduled meeting would be with Paul Johnson. What secrets would be revealed during her exchange with him?

After she dressed, and thought about the day she decided to do some investigating of her own, specifically, research Jack's company, Last Defense. Maybe she could even find out more information about Jack and Michael. So she took out her tablet, but found nothing new on their website. She hadn't felt comfortable doing that at home with Jack looking over her shoulder, and she felt pretty certain there was more to this whole business than he had shared with her.

No more investigating without coffee, though. She left her room and took the elevator down to the lobby where breakfast was being served in the small restaurant. The hostess seated her and wished her a good day in that friendly Texas accent that Lauren was getting used to.

Noticing a stack of local newspapers, she walked over to it and picked one up after ordering a latte and waffles. Sipping the hot, creamy coffee, she scanned the national and local headlines.

Then she saw it. At the bottom of the front page, an article about Last Defense written by a reporter named Elaine Jones caught her eye. The missing plane was the focus of it and if Jack did, indeed, lose his life, the piece explained how his death would affect Last Defense and the pending litigation. Apparently, the company had been involved in much more than one lawsuit through the years. *Hmm. Jack didn't mention that.* She was stunned to find out that Last

Defense had been in more trouble than she thought. The article also briefly discussed the lack of accountability and rules by which Last Defense and companies like it operated. Lauren observed that the writing took on a personal tone, as if the author knew Jack or Michael or had some personal connection with the company.

Lauren finished her breakfast and returned to her hotel room. Pulling off her jeans and top, she changed to the black business suit and high heels she had brought with her in case she needed a more professional look. She then took the elevator down to the first floor and walked briskly out into the lobby. Seeing a young man at the concierge desk with a name plate identifying him as Robert, she smiled. "Robert, could you please call me a taxi?"

"Of course," he responded, looking at her as if she were someone important. His reaction made her happy she'd dressed up. Taking a seat in a nearby plush, comfortable chair, she waited for her ride. After a few minutes, the taxi drove up and Lauren confidently stepped inside.

"Where to, miss?"

"The *Houston Chronicle* building, please," she said.

CHAPTER 12

Apprehensive as she entered the offices of the *Houston Chronicle* in downtown Houston, Lauren felt like a fish out of water in a world very different from her own. Crossing the marble-tiled floor, she wondered whether Elaine Jones would speak with her or if she would be escorted out of the building by a burly security guard. She walked up to the receptionist's desk, and as confidently as she could, she said, "I would like to speak with Elaine Jones."

"Do you have an appointment?"

"No, but could you please tell Ms. Jones that I am a friend of Jack Kelly's from Last Defense? My name is Lauren Reese. I read her article this morning, and I may have some information for her."

Lauren thought that might be a good line for getting in to see Elaine, keeping in mind the goal was that of gaining as much information as possible from her. The rest she would have to adlib. She waited while the receptionist called Elaine.

"She'll be right down. Have a seat. Can I get you anything? Coffee or water?"

"No, thanks. I'm good."

Lauren let out her breath slowly as she sat down in one of the waiting area chairs, incredibly relieved that Elaine would talk with her. Maybe her investigative efforts were going to pay off. Gazing about the waiting area, she noticed a steady flow of reporters coming in and out of the front doors, some carrying laptops and cameras, all in a hurry to get to their next assignment. A slight pang of guilt pricked her because she wasn't at the airport working through the challenges of the last few days. She hoped her boss had been able to find the help that he needed in her absence. She would call him later and find out how everything was going there.

After about ten minutes, a woman impeccably dressed in a well-fitting blouse and skirt that flattered her tall, thin frame, entered the reception area. She had perfectly styled hair, flawless skin, and manicured nails. To say the woman was gorgeous would not be an exaggeration.

"Hello, I'm Elaine," she said as she offered her hand to Lauren.

Lauren stood up, shook Elaine's hand, smiled, and replied, "Hi, I'm Lauren Reese. Thank you for taking the time to speak with me on such short notice."

"Come with me to my office."

Lauren followed Elaine through a set of double doors that required a security card to pass through, then they made their way to an elevator across a room full of cubicles. They vibrated with a constant buzz—television monitors blaring, phones ringing, people talking on phones and tapping on keyboards. They took an elevator up to the third floor. Elaine occupied a spacious office with tall bay windows that allowed a beautiful view of the city, indicating that she was well respected at the paper.

Elaine sat down at her desk and motioned toward several guest chairs facing her. "Please sit down," she said in a warm, friendly voice. Relieved by the welcoming response to her visit, Lauren glanced at the many stacks of paper on Elaine's desk, which included an inbox piled so high that papers were about to spill off of it. Next to the inbox sat a photo of Elaine with a man who had his arm around her, probably a boyfriend or husband. The photo looked like it had been taken on vacation at a tropical location.

Lauren studied Elaine, wondering if she'd made the right decision to speak with her directly. What would she find out about Last Defense?

"You were a friend of Jack's?" Elaine inquired with a slight hint of curiosity in her voice. "Do you live here in Houston?"

"Oh, no," Lauren said. "I live in Aspen, Colorado." Geez, she'd have to tell a lie again about what had brought her so far from home. Since her previous fabrication seemed to work well with Michael Dodson, she figured it would also work with Elaine. "I'm here because Jack had wanted me to look after his affairs if anything ever happened to him." She'd hoped she sounded sufficiently sad about Jack's supposed demise. "We had known each other since college. I read your article in the paper today and knew I needed to talk to you. It was informative and well written, that's why it caught my eye."

"Thank you," Elaine said. Then she hesitated, and her face became softer. "Well, to tell you the truth, I have a personal interest. I dated Jack for a while."

Of course. Who hasn't? Lauren told herself as she gazed at the sultry young woman in front of her. She stayed calm knowing she couldn't reveal the twinge of jealousy she felt.

"I thought I detected a personal tone in your article," Lauren admitted. "Did you think he was in any danger?"

Elaine hesitated for a moment. "Yes, I did. Do you know very much about Jack's business?"

"No. Not beyond what I found online. When he came to Aspen, he was there for vacation, to ski and relax, to forget about his troubles." Lauren didn't feel comfortable about not telling the truth, but in this instance she felt she had no choice.

"In the early days of the Iraq war, and with additional fighting going on in Afghanistan, there weren't enough American troops on the ground," Elaine began. "As things got worse, the need arose for a parallel army to do some essential jobs that couldn't be done because of the military's lack of manpower. This effort turned into a $100 billion dollar industry as the situation deteriorated and a demand for companies like Jack's grew. These companies employed tens of thousands of what we would call mercenaries to protect everything from U.S. officials and generals to shipments of supplies. They now are helping the war effort in Afghanistan, and in the last year more employees of U.S. contractors have been reported killed in Afghanistan than U.S. service members."

"Really? I had no idea."

"That's according to Defense Department statistics. The military is, in effect, privatizing the ultimate sacrifice."

"I have read about these companies. I was surprised that Jack became vice president of a company like that."

Elaine continued, "The bad apples, and there are bad apples, get a lot of press but the majority of people work hard and do a good job. The problem is not the success or the sacrifice of these companies. It is the impunity. The State Department allows them to do as they please with no oversight. Since the private contractors are operating outside the Uniform Code of Military Justice, there are no laws or rules of engagement that govern their behavior. The U.S. military doesn't even know where these companies are at any given time."

"This seems to be a situation that has to change," Lauren reflected.

"Jack and Michael were trying to do just that. They were working on some type of oversight either by the U.S. Government or a commission formed within the industry itself. Michael Dodson has gone to Washington many times to lobby for changes."

"I'm glad to hear that the company is being pro-active."

"The employees of Last Defense are the best. For the most part, they are patriotic and feel that they're doing a worthwhile job, risking their lives for the country they love. They go through an intensive screening process before they are hired."

"So what happened to initiate the lawsuit?" Lauren asked.

"An employee of Last Defense was ambushed and killed in

broad daylight. The family of the employee filed a lawsuit, even though the employee had signed a waiver stating that the Company would not be responsible if he were killed or injured on the job."

"Then what is the basis for the lawsuit?"

"The family thinks the death of their son was the result of gross negligence on the part of the company. The company should have known that the area was unsafe. In fact, the family has suspicions that the ambush may have been planned in advance. Of course, this is confidential and only speculation," Elaine said, suddenly looking as if she were revealing too much information.

"Of course, I realize this is mainly speculation," Lauren said to ease the tension. But the information startled Lauren, and deepened her resolve to find the truth. How could she ever discover what really happened? Was she crazy for thinking she could actually uncover information that might help Jack? At least Elaine was being open. Maybe she just needed to talk to someone. It would be hard to keep all that information bottled up.

Elaine broke the silence. "Lauren, what was it that you came to tell me?"

Lauren decided the truth was best in this situation, in case Elaine knew anything beyond the article she'd written. "I wanted to tell you that Jack told me he was scheduled to meet with a witness who holds crucial information. Jack wanted to hear what the man had to say. He wanted all the facts to come out, no matter what the consequences were. Jack also said that Michael wanted no part of his investigation and demanded that Jack not talk to anyone about the case."

"That sounds like Jack. He had a conscience, and he knew Omar, the man that was killed. Omar was a family friend."

"Who was he, exactly?"

"Omar Kasim was an American citizen of Armenian descent. He spoke Arabic, and several other languages. He was also a graduate of West Point making him a valuable asset to the company. He was promoted quickly, and Jack thought very highly of him. Jack always took the time to know each team member that worked for him. He took a personal interest in them, and wanted to know what was going on in the field. He was obsessed with finding out what really happened to Omar, because he honestly respected and liked him as a co-worker, and, as I mentioned, he was a family friend."

Lauren thought she could see real sadness in Elaine's eyes. She wondered why Jack and Elaine's relationship hadn't become serious. Elaine seemed like a nice person. Not like the materialistic, shallow women that Jack said he always met. She wondered if Jack had been feeding her a line.

"Do you have the name of this witness?" Elaine said, getting back to the business of reporting.

Lauren didn't think it was a good idea to divulge any further information. "No," she said. "Unfortunately, Jack didn't tell me his name. He'd heard that the witness was someone who'd been in Afghanistan the same time Omar was there."

"That's too bad." Elaine looked skeptical, as if she thought Lauren was being evasive.

"It sure would be a great story if I could have an exclusive interview with the witness. Maybe he will contact you if he becomes aware that you are in Houston and handling Jack's affairs. If he does, please give me a call."

"I will. You know, there's also the chance that he will contact you if he's read your article. That's why I wanted to make you aware of him." Lauren was pleased with herself for coming up with that one.

"Thanks." Elaine, now looking uncomfortable, glanced at her watch, as if she were ready to end the meeting.

As Elaine turned her wrist, Lauren noticed a stunning diamond ring on Elaine's left hand.

"What a beautiful ring. Are you engaged?" Lauren asked.

"I am, thank you. The ring isn't exactly what I wanted but it's okay. I wasn't going to wear it until I had it appraised."

Lauren gasped, unable to hide her surprise at the shallow

nature of Elaine's comments. The ring obviously cost a fortune, and the diamond sparkled in the light of the room. Any other woman would be thrilled by it. Lauren immediately began to re-think her opinion of her.

Elaine didn't seem to notice Lauren's reaction, and she stood up to indicate that the meeting was over. "Thank you for coming in," she said as she walked toward the door to escort Lauren out. "Please let me know if you find out anything more about the witness. Here's my card."

"I will. Thank you for taking the time to see me," Lauren said as she took Elaine's business card.

"You're welcome. And good luck with handling Jack's affairs."

As Lauren walked out, she realized that Elaine hadn't inquired about a memorial service for Jack—assuming he was dead—or asked about his dad, which any ex-girlfriend that really did care about him probably would do. Did Elaine only care about landing a good story? Maybe Jack was right about the women he met in his high-flying jet-set life. All of a sudden she shivered, remembering that when she had found Jack at the airport he had turned around and grabbed her, and he'd asked if she was a reporter. Had Elaine done something that hurt Jack at some point? Was it possible that Elaine knew more about this business than she was telling?

The moment Lauren Reese left her office Elaine picked up the phone on her desk and punched in a number. "You'll never guess who just came in to my office," she said to the person on the other end of the line.

CHAPTER 13

Dear Dad,

You will be happy to know that I've decided this is my final mission. I've been thinking about it, and I'm ready to come home for good. I've applied to law school and have been accepted. I can't wait to talk to you about it. It's been a dream of mine for a long time.

This last job was more dangerous than the previous ones I worked on for Last Defense. We escorted tractor-trailers for the military. How about that, Dad? We are protecting the military. We are trying to help stabilize the country, but at the same time we are unofficial and unacknowledged, we're in harm's way every day. It feels a lot different than when I was a solider when my greatest honor was to represent America in the United States Army, just like you did. Well, at least the pay is good and it will more than finance law school.

As far as these private security companies go, Last Defense is the best. The owners always make sure we have the top-of-the-line equipment and supplies, which makes a big difference to our safety and morale. Although, something illegal seems to be going on here, as I mentioned in my last letter.

I have suspicions that there are soldiers selling or using heroin. Drugs are a big problem over here, and I've turned in a report about it. I can't see anyone at Last Defense being involved, but you never know. I'll tell you more about it later, but it's hard to trust anyone over here.

See you soon.

Love, Omar

CHAPTER 14

After leaving the *Houston Chronicle,* Lauren caught a taxi and decided to take Shannon's advice and buy some pepper spray for personal protection. It was only noon, and she had lots of time before meeting with Paul Johnson at five o'clock. When she asked the taxi driver for his advice, he took her to a shop that sold personal security items. Lauren asked him to wait for her while she went into the shop. "I'll only be a few minutes. Leave the meter running," she said.

"No problem—it's your dime," the driver replied in a friendly tone as he took a magazine from the front seat to read while she was gone.

The sales clerk was a muscular young man about six feet tall with tattoos on both arms and a shaved head. He was very polite and tried to convince her that she could only be safe in Houston if she purchased a stun gun. He asked her if she wanted information or a demonstration, which she declined. *A demonstration? On whom? I better get my pepper spray and get out of here,* she thought.

After suffering through more sales pitches for various other weapons, she purchased a container of pepper spray that was small enough to carry in her purse or back jean pocket. She put it in her purse and immediately felt better and decided that even if it was a false sense of security, it was one she needed while in Houston.

"Do you feel safer now?" the taxi driver said with a smile as she got back in the cab.

"Yes, I really do."

"Are you here on business?"

"More or less—but I'm done for the day now, and think I'll just go back to my hotel. Thanks for waiting."

Returning to her room, Lauren called room service and ordered a green salad for lunch, then pulled out her tablet to search for general information about the private security industry and found that these kinds of companies had been around for a long time. She continued to read that the Iraq war brought them out of the shadows for two reasons—the demand for more military manpower and the nature of the conflict. Most of the employees at these companies were former military men who'd become bored after returning home and getting back to mainstream life. These operatives were typically paid quite well for their work, as a multitude of risks could be involved. Some of them thought it a good way to stash away big sums of money. *Interesting stuff,* she thought as she put her tablet away. She now felt well informed about the background of the industry.

As she ate her lunch, which came promptly, she began to feel lonely. She missed the camaraderie with associates and friends at work and the Rocky Mountain beauty she looked at every day in Aspen. The constant rain she'd had to deal with since flying in to Houston was stifling. She wondered what Jack would do now that his career seemed to be falling apart. Where would he go?

Lauren decided to check out the fitness facilities at the hotel. The Hyatt provided top-notch Life Fitness equipment. There was even a 24-hour concierge service to provide workout clothes and GPS armbands to help runners monitor their heart rate and distance, as well as their way back to the hotel. Although she couldn't imagine people running in the summer in Houston with its stifling heat and humidity, or even now, in the rain, she thought it was nice of the hotel to offer the service.

She decided instead to just go for a dip in the hotel's swimming pool, proud of herself for remembering to pack her suit. She needed to burn off some of the stress that was building up in anticipation of her meeting with Paul Johnson. *Is this meeting dangerous? Did someone try to kill Jack to keep him from meeting with Paul?*

The water was cool and refreshing. Except for a woman with two small children, she had the pool and fitness area to herself. After the swim she treated herself to the sauna and a soak in the hot tub, then returned to her room completely relaxed.

After showering, she got dressed for her meeting, putting on a pair of casual slacks and a fairly low-cut knit top she'd bought at the hotel gift shop for the occasion. She wanted to look like a typical lounge patron and wear something comfortable that would make Paul feel at ease. Almost time for the meeting, she sat at the desk in the foyer of the suite, watching the clock and reading the hotel guest reference book. She jumped at the sound of her phone ringing. *I must be more nervous than I think I am.* She picked it up immediately.

It was Jack. "Lauren, how are you doing?" he asked with concern in his voice.

"I'm fine. How about you? Staying out of trouble? Have you been skiing?" Lauren hoped that her voice wasn't trembling, she didn't want to alert Jack that she was anxious about the meeting."

"No, I'm a dead man, remember? I didn't want to press my luck about not being recognized again. They're still flashing my picture on the television news stories."

"Smart. It would be better to stay put."

"What have you been doing all day? I thought you would call me."

"I've kept busy. Don't laugh, but I went into a gun shop and came out with pepper spray."

"I wouldn't laugh. I think that's a very good idea. Keep it in your pocket at all times."

"I went for a swim and a sauna. This is a wonderful hotel. You know they offer a GPS service for guests that want to go for a run?"

"I can't imagine anyone wanting to go for a run in Houston unless they're running away from the muggers."

Lauren laughed. "I'm sure it's not that bad here, Jack. Anyway, I also watched a movie on HBO. It's been a relaxing trip. I owe you for the opportunity to have a short break from work." She didn't want to tell him about Elaine Jones or that she was researching Last Defense. She also didn't want to give him the impression that she didn't trust him.

"Did you get a chance to go to my condo and pick up my mail?"

"No, I thought I would do that tomorrow before I left for the airport. In case today's mail came in late."

"Okay, I guess you're right. Wednesday's mail might be there too when you check it. I'm interested to see if I've received anything important."

"I'll call you and let you know what I find," she promised.

"Are you ready for your meeting with Paul?"

"Yes, I'm a little nervous but I'm okay. I'll call you right afterwards, of course."

"Okay, please do, and good luck. Thanks again for doing this. I owe you one. Actually, I owe you a lot. How can I ever repay you? You're a one-of-a-kind woman, Lauren."

Lauren was stunned, surprised by Jack's display of heartfelt gratitude. "Forget it. I'm enjoying myself here. I'll be on my way back home tomorrow. It's been a fun trip. I'd better hang up now or I'll be late for my meeting with Paul."

"Okay, then. Bye—and be safe. Take your pepper spray."

At 4:50 p.m. Lauren left her room to take the elevator down to the Prairie Schooner, the hotel lounge that was located off to the side of the lobby. She walked in and sat down at a small table in a corner, facing the entrance. When the waitress came by, she ordered a margarita. The drink came in a wide glass with a salted rim, a lime wedge, and a straw.

A well-dressed gentleman in a tan business suit walked up to the empty seat across the table from Lauren and said to her, "Is this seat taken?"

Lauren knew from the physical description of Paul that it wasn't him. She blushed and said, "Yes, I'm waiting for someone. Thanks anyway."

The man smiled at her. "Lucky guy," he said and then he walked over toward the bar and took a seat, glancing over toward Lauren occasionally.

Sipping the drink slowly through the straw, she looked around. The bar was more crowded than she'd expected. The muted music sounded like contemporary rock. Scanning the patrons, she saw a lot of businessmen, some in groups and some alone, sitting at tables and bar stools around the darkly lit room that was decorated in a maritime theme. A large ship's wheel hung on the wall next to her, and she could see ship models placed along one of the walls. A young couple sat at the adjacent table, drinking margaritas and eating chips and salsa. Lauren looked at her watch. It was ten minutes after five, and she was starting to worry that Paul was not going to show up.

Then she noticed a man standing at the entrance of the bar matching the description that Paul had given her. He looked nervous and apprehensive as he scanned the happy hour patrons. When he finally entered, Lauren stood up and waved to him. He saw her and started to walk toward her, but then looked like he was having second thoughts. Suddenly, he turned and abruptly left. Lauren looked around but couldn't figure out any explanation for his behavior and she couldn't get through the crowded bar quickly enough to follow him.

A huge wave of disappointment and confusion swept over her. This meeting was the entire reason for her trip to Houston. The last thing she wanted to do was disappoint Jack. She sat down at her table for another twenty minutes, hoping Paul would return or text her on her cell phone, but then surrendered to the idea that something must have scared him off. After paying for her drink, she left and went back to her room. She'd have to call Jack and tell him the bad news.

CHAPTER 15

As Lauren entered her hotel room and placed her purse on the desk by the door, she caught a glimpse of something moving in the reflection of the mirror above the desk. Her heart raced as she realized she was not alone in her room. When she turned around, she saw Michael Dodson standing over by the loveseat. On the coffee table sat a bottle of wine and two glasses.

Lauren struggled to regain her composure. *Don't these guys ever knock?* Her body went into "fight or flight" response mode and her pulse raced. She instinctively put her hand on her purse which contained the pepper spray, knowing that she had some sort of protection at her disposal if she needed it. It was bad enough that Paul had run off, but now she had to deal with an unexpected visitor in her hotel room. She tried to sound like she was in control of the situation but failed. "How did you . . . ?" she managed to stutter, looking squarely at Michael to see what his intentions were.

"This is our company suite and I have a master key," he said.

"Of course you do," Lauren said in a slightly sarcastic tone as she realized by his demeanor that he was not there to harm her. She calmed down. "Most people knock. But you aren't most people, are you?"

"I'm sorry if I frightened you, I wanted to surprise you," Michael said with a gentle smile on his face, his brown eyes alert and warm. "I just came in to bring you these." He pointed to a bouquet of flowers on the desk and the bottle of wine on the coffee table. "I was getting ready to leave, but you caught me. I realized that I wasn't very welcoming when we met yesterday and wanted to show you some real Texas hospitality."

Lauren walked over to the desk and studied the beautiful bouquet of pink roses, Peruvian lilies, and asters. A small note that said "Have dinner with me" was attached to the arrangement.

Obviously this guy has an enormous amount of clout in this town. I should have known this was a company suite by the military-themed artwork and the military magazines on the coffee table. Note to self: stop being so naïve.

"How nice," she said, thinking it would be best to oblige him. She looked at the bottle of wine. He'd already uncorked it, and she could smell the bouquet of a fine, rich Cabernet Sauvignon.

Sitting down, Michael poured two glasses of wine. "Seriously, I want you to feel welcome, and I want to express my gratitude that you have come to Houston," he said. I'm sure that Jack would want to thank you himself if he were here. Why didn't you come to the office today?"

Lauren noticed his athletic build. He looked very handsome in a tailor-made black suit complemented with a shimmering red tie. And again, she noticed that he spoke with a very slight British accent. She caught herself staring at him and felt a little embarrassed as her cheeks turned pink. Still a bit taken aback that he would dare to enter her hotel room without her permission, she sat down across from him on the couch and decided to play along.

"I'm sorry I didn't make it to the office today," she said, not wanting to give away the fact that she had no intention of going to the office.

"I want to help you in any way I can to settle Jack's affairs and his estate," he said in a conciliatory tone. "As far as I know, Jack didn't have any siblings, and his mother passed away from cancer a few years ago."

"That's correct. He had no immediate family except for his dad."

"I think he had a stepbrother, but he died, too, in a construction accident."

Lauren was unaware that Jack had another sibling. He had never mentioned him. She didn't want her surprise to show on her face so she composed herself quickly. So, Jack was practically alone in the world, just like she was. She picked up one of the glasses in front of her and took a sip. The wine tasted as rich as it looked and smelled. *This man does have class, even though he is a little bold and assuming.*

"I want you to come to Last Defense tomorrow," Michael continued, gazing at her intently. "And I'd also be happy to show you around Houston."

"Thank you, I would love to come to the office tomorrow. I'm leaving in the afternoon, but I can stop in before I go."

She didn't plan on visiting the Last Defense offices but thought she should keep up the ruse of being interested in Jack's company. She couldn't tell Michael that she only came to Houston to meet with Paul Johnson.

"You're leaving so soon?" Michael looked surprised.

She nodded. "I have to get back home. As I mentioned before, I work at the Aspen airport and my boss really needs me. It was hard to get away for these couple of days, but now I can do what has to be done from there. I can always return to Houston if necessary."

"In that case we do need to go to dinner tonight. I know a great restaurant close by where we can talk and get to know each other better."

Lauren figured there would be a catch. It looked like Michael had his eye on her as a potential single female who was a bit vulnerable at this point. Either that or he wanted to find out how much she knew about the company and Jack.

Suddenly, Lauren realized that if she didn't call Jack soon, he would be calling her, which would make for an awkward situation. She could turn off her cell phone, but she had no way to control the ringing of the phone on the desk if Jack tried to contact her through the hotel switchboard. Also, he might find out that she was in the company suite if he called the hotel. She sipped more of the wine and told Michael she would love to take him up on his dinner offer. Since she didn't have any dinner plans, why not? *What would it hurt? It could be fun and informative to find out more about the president of Last Defense.*

Michael took a drink of his wine. "Tell me more about yourself and your relationship with Jack. I'm guessing you were lovers."

Lauren choked on her sip of wine at the nonchalant manner Michael used when probing for personal details about her life.

"Well, at least you're direct. We were college sweethearts. He left to go to Harvard Business School but we kept in touch. You know how you never forget your first love. I'm not sure if it's the memories or the innocent, exciting times of our lives that we can't bear to part with."

"I do know, although my first love divorced me. That was the hardest thing I have ever had to go through. Worse than anything that has ever happened to me in the field."

"I'm sorry to hear about your divorce. Why not tell me about your military experience, instead?"

"I was a British commando in the Special Air Service. I fought some combat missions and ran undercover operations in areas of the Middle East and Africa. After I got out, I wasn't able to leave the action behind, and so, when I met Jack we pooled our resources and started Last Defense. We're a company that provides overseas private security contracting for all types of clients."

"I see." She already knew this from her research and her meeting with Elaine, but she didn't want to let on that she had inside information.

"Jack and I got along well together, and since he didn't have a military background, he handled the business end of things. He had a solid financial background and an MBA—smart guy. He also was starting to get more involved in operations. It was a good relationship for a while."

"What happened?"

"I think his inexperience in the field got in the way of his decisions. Most of our employees are highly trained former military personnel. The adrenaline, the camaraderie, well, Jack just didn't get it. In the field, everyone has to watch out for everyone else. It's not just about money."

Lauren chose to disregard the negative insinuations Michael had just made about Jack and decided this was a good opportunity to find out everything she could about Michael. She inquired, "Do you still go out in the field?"

"Yes, but I haven't been in for a while. We're shifting our focus to other lines of business, including international training and air support in places like Africa."

After changing the conversation to lighter topics, like the weather and living in Houston, Lauren started to really worry about Jack calling her cell phone or the phone in her room. That would blow her cover and everything else. It was almost six o'clock. "Well, should we go to dinner?" she asked, hoping to make a quick escape before she had to think of an excuse as to why she wouldn't be answering a ringing phone.

"Yes, I made reservations for six o'clock," he said with a charming smile. "I was hoping you would accept my invitation."

She looked down at her casual blouse and slacks, and then at his elegant suit. "I didn't bring formal attire with me, so I don't have anything to wear that would complement your outfit."

"I hope you don't mind that I took the liberty of buying you something. I guessed you were a size eight."

Lauren noticed that Michael had brought a bag with him embossed with the hotel's signature logo on it. He gave it to her, then sat back and watched her open it. Inside, wrapped in elegant tissue paper, she found a crinkle silk chiffon black evening dress.

With her fingers gently gliding over it, she couldn't help but smile. It had a smocked waist, flutter sleeves, and a flowing feminine skirt that ended with gentle ruffles at the knee.

"Yes, this is my size. You have good taste. The dress is beautiful, Michael. Thank you."

"You will have to thank the sales clerk for doing her job so well. I thought you would like it."

"I'll try it on, right now," she said as she went into the bedroom of the suite, taking her purse with her so that she could turn off her cell phone. She was surprised someone could be so presumptuous, but she was also pleased that Michael showed interest in her. After being without a man for such a long time, it was exciting to have two men in her life at once.

A few minutes later she came out of the bedroom looking stunning in the gorgeous dress. The black heels she brought complemented it perfectly.

"You look beautiful," Michael said as he stood up to leave.

"Thank you. You can be my personal shopper any time."

CHAPTER 16

Lauren grabbed her purse and raincoat, then followed Michael out to the hall and into the elevator, where they quickly reached ground level. Briefly taking her hand, he steered her into the direction of the lobby, then outside to a private parking area and an impressive black BMW sports car, the kind of car she'd imagined that he drove. She was enjoying the romance of a date, something she had not had in a while. Had she really gotten in such a rut, coping with her personal tragedy, to the point where she had forgotten about having fun with the opposite sex?

"The restaurant is only a few minutes from here," Michael said, opening the door for her and then settling into the driver's seat. Easing the car out of the parking spot, he drove to Gerard's, an upscale establishment, only five minutes away from the hotel.

Upon entering, Lauren found it to be intimate and quiet, the atmosphere dark and romantic. The hostess sat them at a private table toward the back of the main room, away from any other patrons. As the waiter came by to take their order, Michael asked Lauren if he could place it for her.

"Sure. You've eaten here before so you know the menu. I trust you to select something wonderful."

Michael ordered the special prime rib dinner for both of them and another bottle of Napa Valley Cabernet Sauvignon. The waiter brought the wine to the table and opened it with skill and finesse, then asked Michael to taste it. Michael approved, and the waiter poured the wine into two crystal glasses.

While waiting for their entrees, they each shared more information about themselves. Lauren told Michael about her career, about losing her parents, and all about her home in Aspen, surprising herself by being so open with him. *Why do I feel so comfortable with this man? Why am I telling this stranger, this possible dangerous man, things about my personal life?*

"Have you ever been to Aspen?" she asked him.

"No, I haven't. Why don't you invite me there sometime?"

What a flirt. "Do you ski?"

"I can learn. Maybe you could teach me."

Lauren laughed. "I probably wouldn't be the best teacher. The good instructors are teaching all the movie stars and celebrities, which I'm sure isn't easy."

"No, I wouldn't think that would be. Where exactly is Aspen?"

"Aspen is pretty much in the middle of the state of Colorado. Most people think that Denver is in the middle of the state. Some even think that Denver is in the mountains because it's known as the "mile high city." But Denver is actually located north and east, in what is known as the "front range." Aspen is on the western slope and Denver is on the eastern slope. Slope refers to the Continental Divide, which is the line that divides the flow of water either toward the Pacific Ocean or the Atlantic Ocean. The divide runs through Colorado."

"I see. You should be a tour guide."

"Speaking of that, I have to mention our luscious Colorado wines. I'll send you a bottle. Some of them are world class and can effectively compete with California and European wines. You will be surprised."

"I'm sold. Send me a bottle."

"I hope you didn't mind the geography lesson. Please tell me more about yourself."

Michael then shared stories of his military career. Lauren had to admire his courage and sense of duty. He also seemed to be as modest as he was heroic. He told her about one particularly dangerous assignment involving dynamite and a drunken diplomat. Time flew as the two drank wine and ate a perfectly cooked prime rib dinner.

Lauren was amazed that she got along with Michael so well. Their evening out seemed far removed from the plane crash and Jack waiting at her house in Aspen. She wondered briefly why Michael was spending time with her, and why he was being so nice. Maybe he was suspicious of her motives. Could he somehow know that her plan was to meet with Paul Johnson and find out everything she could about the lawsuit? Was she in danger? She put that thought out of her mind, and resumed laughing and talking with him. *How could he possibly know why I'm really here?*

"What drew you to this life, the military, and then private contracting?" Lauren asked. "The adventure, the sense of duty, or the money?"

"All of the above. The camaraderie from working with other soldiers in the field. The adrenaline rush from the action."

"Were you ever worried about being killed?"

"I was more worried about being captured. I worry about my reputation. If I'm captured and end up on national TV, how embarrassing would that be? So you have to fight to the death. There's no way I ever would have been captured alive."

"I see. Can you sense when danger is imminent?"

"Yes, you do develop a sixth sense."

Lauren was going to ask about Omar and the lawsuit but didn't want to spoil the mood. She wanted to dedicate this evening to find out about Michael. Who was this man? What part did he play in the company, and was he involved in any way with the tragedy that happened?"

The restaurant provided an open area for dancing, and after

they finished with dinner Michael asked her to dance. Their eyes met, and Lauren felt a connection with this man to whom she was opening up to more and more.

As he took her into his arms for a slow dance, his strong muscular body pressed against hers. Desire surged through her. How long had it been since she danced like this? Senior prom, maybe? She'd forgotten how romantic and sensual dancing could be. The hint of danger and intrigue surrounding Michael made it more so. She wished the night would never end.

Then her sensible side took over. *What am I thinking? I need to get back to the hotel room where Jack is probably frantically trying to call. Here I am, dancing with Michael. The enemy. Or is he?*

After another dance, this one less romantically enticing, she told Michael that she was tired and should probably get back to her hotel room. He obliged and gave the young man at the front entrance the ticket to retrieve his car from valet parking. It stopped raining and the short trip back to the Hyatt took only a few minutes. As they pulled up to her hotel, Lauren said, "You can just drop me off—no need to park and walk me to my door."

"Don't you trust me?" Michael asked, giving her a wry smile.

Lauren looked at Michael and smiled back. "Maybe I don't trust myself," she said, surprised she could be such a tease.

"Do you want me to pick you up in the morning on my way to the office?"

She shook her head. "No. That's all right. I'd like to take a taxi, if you don't mind. What time should I be there?"

"Any time in the morning would be fine. Here's my card that lists the address. None of the taxis will have any trouble finding the building. We're on a secure floor, so just tell the security guard in the lobby that you're there to see me at my invitation, and he'll ring up to the office. Someone will come down and get you."

"Thank you for a wonderful evening," Lauren said, sincerely meaning the words.

"It was my pleasure."

They looked at each other with longing eyes. When she leaned forward to hug him, he kissed her.

Lauren could feel the blood rush to her cheeks.

It was a passionate kiss, deep and full of longing. Lauren was not prepared for the sensuality of the date and the kiss. The danger of the situation made Michael's kiss more enticing, and she could feel her knees grow weak. Instead of exiting the door at that moment, which she thought would be the sensible thing to do, she kissed him again. Could he tell that she longed for more love and passion in her life? There they were, making out in his car, like teenagers after a date.

"Are you sure you don't want me to come up?" Michael whispered.

Looking at him, a surge of desire nearly overwhelmed her, and she realized that she really needed to leave before she forgot who she was, where she was, and what she was doing here. She politely declined his offer, released her seat belt, and opened the car door.

If only this was a different time and a different place.

Gingerly, she exited the car and waved goodbye, entered the hotel lobby, then took the elevator up to her room.

As she stepped in, the phone on the desk was ringing, just as she had expected. She answered it right away, knowing it would be Jack.

"Finally," he said after she answered the phone, anger and concern in his voice. "This is my third phone call. You aren't answering your cell phone, either. Are you all right? What happened? Where have you been?"

She told him about Paul Johnson's mysterious behavior. Jack seemed concerned, but he didn't think Paul's quick exit had anything to do with Lauren. "If you didn't talk to Paul, why didn't you call me sooner? I've been incredibly worried about you. Where have you been?"

Lauren didn't want to tell him about Michael, but realized that she couldn't make up a believable story about where she had been all evening. Lying and deceiving people were new to her, and she was weary of it already. "I went out to dinner with Michael Dodson. He showed up at my hotel room and I couldn't refuse. I decided it was an opportunity to find out more about what's going on." She hesitated to tell him more than that, especially about Michael's appearance in her locked hotel room and his romantic overtures, not to mention the passionate kisses. Jack must not have found out that she was staying in the company suite. If he'd known he would have mentioned it. She just hoped that she didn't sound too excited about the evening.

She felt a little guilty. Jack seemed deeply troubled that she'd spent the evening with Michael.

"What? You're kidding, right? He could be a murderer. What if he finds out why you're really there, Lauren? He might have a tail on Paul, and if so, he's finding out right now that Paul went to the hotel to meet with you. I'm concerned about your safety. Please, just take the next plane back to Colorado."

Lauren could hear the desperation in his voice. She thought she heard glass breaking in the background and could imagine him pacing the floor as he talked to her. She knew the last thing Jack wanted was for Michael to hurt her, mislead her, or romantically sweep her off of her feet. Not necessarily in that order.

"I'll just take the three o'clock flight back to Colorado that I've scheduled for tomorrow. I'll check your mail in the morning and then drop by the Last Defense office to pack up your personal items and pictures. I want to make it look like I'm really here to act as the executor of your estate and have your best interests in mind. I don't feel like I'm in any danger, Jack, so don't worry. I have a sixth sense about danger." This really wasn't true. Michael had told her something of the sort about when he was in the field. It sounded good, so she used his line now.

"You're planning on going to the office? Don't tell me. Michael invited you, right?"

"Well, yes."

"Lauren, do you really think it's a coincidence that Paul didn't meet with you at the bar, but Michael showed up at your hotel?"

"Good point. I didn't think of that."

"Lauren, remember what Carl told you about sabotage? What are you thinking?"

"Yes, I know. But I did come here to complete a mission." *My God, now I'm even sounding like Michael Dodson.*

Lauren felt faint when she remembered the gravity of the situation with the missing plane. She sank down on the chair at the desk

"Your mission is over. Come home," Jack said in a deep, earnest tone.

She could visualize the serious look on his face. "I'll be extra careful, Jack. This will be my only chance to find out something that could help you. I promise to keep things strictly business tomorrow and just gather your personal things. I'll see if I can find out anything of interest, and then I'll catch a plane home."

"Strictly business? Why do you say that? What happened tonight between the two of you?"

Lauren hadn't meant for that to slip out. She didn't want Jack to know about the romantic nature of the evening. She blushed and was happy that Jack wasn't there to see her face turn slightly red. "Just a dinner, Jack."

"Don't go the office tomorrow," Jack pleaded.

"I have an idea," she said, changing the subject. "I'll send another text to Paul. Maybe he'll write back and say why he didn't talk to me at the bar. I hope that I hear from him and can still meet with him, but if not, I'll just plan on leaving tomorrow afternoon. If you insist, I won't go to the office. I'll pick up your mail and go straight to the airport and try to get on an earlier flight to Denver. Don't worry. Really."

"Okay, make sure to call me on my cell phone and let me know what's going on."

"I promise. I'll keep you posted from now on."

"Just be careful. If anything happened to you . . ."

"Don't even think that. I'll be in Aspen again before you know it. I'm homesick. I even miss angry, tired travelers barking at me about their delayed or cancelled flights."

"All right. Goodnight and I'll see you soon."

"Goodnight, Jack. And don't worry!"

Lauren had been unable to convince Jack that she was safe. He sounded disturbed as he said goodnight, and she wondered if this was all concern for her safety or if some of his angst was jealousy. She did a check of all the closets and the bathroom, then promptly locked the dead bolt and the security latch on her door to make sure she didn't encounter any more unexpected visitors who had their own master keys.

After they hung up, Jack looked down at the shattered water glass on the hardwood floor of Lauren's house. The glass had fallen out of his hand when he'd heard where Lauren had been all evening.

As he cleaned up the mess, he wondered if Lauren would be able to figure out everything that was going on. As quickly as possible, he had to get to Houston.

CHAPTER 17

Wednesday morning, after a sound sleep, Lauren awoke to the wake-up call she had requested. The annoying ring disturbed another dream. This time it was a sensual dream. In it, she'd been making love to Michael Dodson. Hmm. *Maybe a cold shower this morning might be what I need.* Even though she felt embarrassed about the dream, she decided not to let it bother her and attributed it to the stress of her "out of routine" situation. All this testosterone coming at her was a shock to her system, considering she had been in a reclusive rut for a while. Her intention was to ease into dating again slowly. Although, she did have to admit, she wondered what it would be like to make love to Michael Dodson. *How would he feel and taste and move? Would foreplay be gentle like his slow dancing, or more passionate like making out in the front seat of his car?*

Time to get up. This morning she had to pick up Jack's mail and then hightail it out of Houston. The disappointment she felt because she hadn't heard from Paul was weighing on her mind. This was her last day in Houston, and therefore the last chance to meet with him and get the file he wanted to turn over to Jack. Still . . . no messages on her phone. Why hadn't he at least sent her a text to explain? He must have changed his mind about turning over the file. But why?

Her thoughts returned to Jack. Could they possibly rekindle their relationship? Again, she wondered if he was just using her, or did he really care about her? He did seem genuinely worried that she'd been with Michael last night, and she'd noticed some jealousy in his voice.

And then there was Michael. What interest did he have in her? Why was he so willing to go out of his way to impress her? That was the biggest mystery, she decided, as she dried herself off and got dressed after her brief shower. Will he be disappointed when she doesn't show up at the office today? *I'll call him from the airport and explain that I had to get back to work urgently.*

After breakfast at the hotel's quaint café, she packed up her suitcase and checked out, glad to be leaving the company suite, which she didn't feel completely comfortable in. Again, she asked Robert to call for a taxi, which took all of one minute, as there was already a cab waiting out front. The helpful driver took her suitcase and stowed it on the backseat next to where she sat. Anxious to see where Jack lived, she didn't learn much about the city during the short ride. It was raining again, and all of the buildings looked dark and dreary. The weather was beginning to get to her.

She found her thoughts focusing on the brilliant Aspen sunshine she was missing, and Jack who was waiting at her house. She hoped that he had figured out what to do about her failure to talk to the mysterious Paul Johnson.

Arriving at Jack's condo, she found the mailboxes, which were in a designated building just as Jack had described. Taking out his mail key and inserting it in the slot of cubicle number twelve as he had instructed her, a few pieces of advertising mail and bills spilled out from the overfilled box onto the floor. Then she saw it.

Standing out among the mail was a letter from Ali Kasim, the father of Omar Kasim, addressed to Jack and marked "Personal and Confidential." She gathered the spilled mail and, except for the letter from Ali Kasim, put the stack in her suitcase's outside pocket when she got back into the taxi. Safe inside the backseat, she opened the letter and read it in silence as the rain fell down upon the taxi traveling on the freeway toward the airport.

Dear Jack,

Several months ago I asked you to look into the circumstances surrounding the death of my son, Omar. I told you that Omar wrote several letters to me of concern about illegal activities going on in the area where he was assigned. You told me that you were investigating the situation. I have tried not to be anxious, but it is hard. Omar was our only son. We feel helpless as we wait to hear about the results of an investigation and if anyone will ever be brought to justice. We do not feel that he was killed by insurgents, but rather, as a result of his inquiries into heroin use and drug smuggling among American contractors and soldiers. I have appealed to you not only as the vice president of Last Defense, but also as a family friend.

Omar wrote to us the weekend before the ambush and said that he was concerned about being stationed in a remote and dangerous area near Pakistan. He didn't know why he was sent there and felt that there might be a traitor in his midst. He downplayed it, of course. That's how he was, saying that rumors abounded in their type of work and that you couldn't worry about them or you'd never get anything done. Omar said that he didn't know whom he could trust and didn't know what to do.

I have gone through all of Omar's letters with a fine-tooth comb, and I believe I have an idea who is responsible for the death of my son. Something that Omar mentioned stands out in my mind. I would like to talk to you about it to reveal what my suspicions are, before I go to the authorities and my lawyer. Please contact me. I await word from you.

Ali Kasim

Lauren's heart beat faster. The reality of her dangerous situation hit her hard. *Omar thought there was a traitor in his midst. The words of a man killed in an ambush. As if their mission wasn't dangerous enough. Seen enemies and unseen enemies. How could these guys stand a chance?*

Reading the letter from Ali gave Lauren a deeper personal

connection to the case. She wanted to find out what happened to Omar and why. She knew now that she couldn't leave Houston until she discovered the truth. How could she arrange to meet with Ali? She wouldn't be going to the airport, now or later today. *What is Ali suggesting in the letter?* If she read it one way, it seemed to be implicating Jack. *Oh my God, what have I gotten myself into?*

Taking out her cell phone, she called the Hyatt to make reservations for another room—not the company suite, but her own room paid for with her own credit card. She didn't feel comfortable with Last Defense paying for this room. In an accommodating tone, the hotel clerk said that she could check in early, at any time. *Wonderful, I can check in now and won't have to lug my suitcase around. This is all falling into place as if it was meant to be.* Explaining her situation to the taxi driver, he was more than happy to take her back to the Hyatt to check in again.

Next she called the airline to cancel her flight to Denver. Attempting to call Jack to tell him of her plans to spend another day in Houston, she felt a little relieved that she wasn't able to connect with him. She left a message, telling him of her plans to stay another day. *That's better. He would just try to talk me out of it anyway.*

With clumsy hands, she nervously called Ali Kasim's phone number that was printed on his personal stationary. She had decided she would use the same tact that she used with Elaine and Michael—her rehearsed explanation of her presence in Houston.

"Hello," a woman's voice answered on the other end of the line.

"Hello, may I speak to Ali Kasim?"

"He's not available. Who's calling, please?"

"I'm a friend. A friend of Jack Kelly's. I would like to talk to Ali. When will he be available?"

"He's out of town. He'll be back tomorrow."

"Are you his wife?"

"I'm his daughter. He'll be back tomorrow. Would you like to leave a message?"

"No message. I'll call back tomorrow. Thanks."

Disappointed, Lauren put her cell phone back into her purse. The taxi pulled into the registration area of the Hyatt. Kindly, the driver helped Lauren remove her suitcase out of the taxi, and she rolled it into the lobby where the clerk remembered her and was friendly and helpful.

"Here you go, miss," he said as he handed her the room key.

"Thank you."

In a flash, Lauren went up to her room, which turned out to be much smaller than the company suite. After dropping off her suitcase and quickly changing into her business suit, which she thought was more appropriate, considering where she had planned to visit next, she came back down to the lobby and climbed into the taxi."

She took out Michael's card and gave the driver the address printed on it. It was a short trip before the taxi dropped her off in front of the office building, at half past ten. After paying the driver for the fare, thanking him for his patience, and giving him a generous tip, she hurried into the lobby, announcing herself to the security guard that she was there, by appointment, to see Michael Dodson at Last Defense. The security guard rang the office, and shortly afterward a young woman in her mid-twenties, with short blonde hair, blue eyes and very attractive, stepped out of the elevator and walked toward Lauren. Kate was exactly what Lauren expected. She fit the part of a representative of a highly successful company and spoke in a professional and sympathetic manner.

"You must be Lauren. I'm so sorry about Jack. I haven't been able to sleep just thinking about it. I know you were a friend of his. You must be devastated, as we all are here."

"The last few days have been difficult," Lauren admitted truthfully.

"I'm Kate. It's very nice to meet you. Michael is expecting you."

"It is nice to meet you, too, Kate."

Lauren followed her into the elevator where she took out a special key that allowed the elevator to stop at the twenty-sixth floor. They walked down a corridor. Using another card key, they entered, through large double doors, into a luxurious office space with a spacious reception area where Kate worked. Next, she directed Lauren into a corner office with glass panels on the front wall facing the corridor, and full-length windows at the back, offering an excellent view of the city. It was decorated in a western style, and Michael sat in a black leather chair behind an expansive oak desk. As Lauren walked through the open door, he looked up from his computer.

Extending his hand he said, "Hello again." She noticed a glint in his eye as she shook his hand, and his attractive face broke into a smile. He wore another expensive tailor made suit, this one was light gray. "Have a seat. How do you like your coffee?"

"With cream and sugar," she responded, sitting down directly across from Michael's desk in one of the most comfortable leather chairs she'd felt in a long time. What a beautiful office and welcoming response she was receiving. She was glad she'd brought her business suit along on the trip. It gave her confidence knowing that she fit in with the culture of the company.

Michael nodded to Kate, and the woman left the room then soon returned with her coffee in a china cup on a silver tray with cream and sugar in matching silver containers.

"Can I get you anything else?"

"No, I'm fine," she said and reached for the cup and saucer. Kate left the room, Lauren looked at Michael as she used a silver spoon to place sugar and cream into her coffee. "Thanks for dinner last night and the dress. I enjoyed the evening. You do know how to make a girl feel welcome," she said. *Does Michael have a romantic interest in me—or is this business? I guess I'll find out now.*

"You're welcome, Lauren. It was my pleasure."

Then, deciding to get straight to the point, in an even voice she said, "I've heard that there's a lawsuit filed against Last Defense from an employee's family, an employee that was killed in the field."

The look on Michael's face told her that she was out of line with the question. His demeanor seemed to change.

"I'm only asking because it might affect Jack's estate," she quickly added to ease the tension and give her an excuse for being so inquisitive.

Sipping his own cup of coffee, Michael searched Lauren's face.

"I'm upset about Jack, too," he said after a long pause. "It's hard now to do both his job and my job, so I've given a fair share of Jack's responsibilities to Andy Harris, he's head of security and the operations manager here. I've also assigned Joseph Chen, another key employee who handles all recruitment, oversees some computer programming and is now acting as CFO in Jack's absence. Luckily, Joe has a background in finance also. I trust them, which is saying something. It's hard for me to trust anyone after what I've been through in my personal life."

"Yes, your divorce. I remember." Lauren glanced at all the papers on his desk. "You're handling a lot right now. And here I am, interrupting your busy day. I don't mean to be intrusive."

"No, not at all, I'm glad you're here. I invited you because I wanted to see you again, and I wanted you to see where Jack worked. I thought you might be interested. He was a vital part of this company."

"I know."

The look on Michael's face became very serious and foreboding. He continued speaking.

"Recently, however, I had begun doubting Jack's abilities and wondering whether he was helping the company or hindering it. I wasn't able to fully understand Jack wanting to investigate the Afghanistan tragedy on his own and his unwillingness to let the lawyers and our public relations firm handle everything associated with the tragic events surrounding Omar Kasim's death. Jack was reluctant to follow the normal procedure. Numerous mechanisms have always been implemented to minimize, and even eliminate, accidents in the field. Everyone has a job to do, and procedures are always followed. As far as I am concerned, Last Defense has done nothing wrong."

Michael studied Lauren's face. "I didn't want to tell you this, Lauren, but I think it's possible that Jack may ultimately be responsible for Omar Kasim's death through an error in oversight and planning." He said this, trying to gauge her reaction. "I think that could be why he wanted to settle the lawsuit. Keep it out of court. He said that he was handling the investigation on his own."

Lauren's world came crashing down. The shock of this new possibility rocked her to the core. She remembered her suspicions regarding the interpretation of Ali Kasim's vague letter. She felt hollow, almost losing the grip on her coffee cup. "Really," she responded slowly. "I didn't think Jack was that kind of man," she managed to say in a weak and strained voice. "I thought that he really cared about his employees."

"I thought he did, too. But unexpected things happen, especially in the field."

"Maybe he knew something that you didn't," Lauren offered.

"I'm going to fight this lawsuit. I feel bad about Omar, but our reputation is at stake. We employ a public relations firm, and they are handling the press on this matter. The lawyers are handling all the legal aspects. We've got over one hundred employees, and I can assure you that all of them are handpicked and their backgrounds thoroughly investigated. We use psychology oriented software in our screening process to test each individual's innate tendencies. Our employees are the best. It was Jack's project and his planning that resulted in Omar Kasim being killed during an unexpected attack. And I don't think he would have let it happen if he he'd known he could have prevented it."

"I see," Lauren managed, barely able to respond.

"I'm sorry for you to hear this."

Lauren felt the blood drain from her face as she tried to process this information. Was it possible that she was being naïve about everything? She came to the realization that there was a part of life, dangerous and evil, that she just didn't understand. Those things didn't exist in her cozy, sheltered world in Aspen.

Lauren gazed blankly at Michael. He must have realized that he sounded defensive and that she was probably in shock to hear his suspicions, so he used a lighter tone when he said, "I can see this is upsetting you. I don't know how Jack's estate will be affected by the lawsuit and the criminal investigation. It would probably be best if you have his lawyer contact our lawyer. They can handle it. That's why we pay them, right?"

"Criminal investigation?"

"Yes. Some crazy prosecutor will be looking at us all personally. Thank God we have a good legal team. No need for you to get involved. What did Jack tell you about this?"

"He told me nothing. I've read about the lawsuit in the papers."

"Don't worry, Lauren. I'm sure you'll feel better once you talk with Jack's lawyer. I hear he's one of the best."

Lauren was staring off into space, trying to process this new information.

"Would you like to see Jack's office?" Michael asked after a few long moments.

"Huh? Oh, yes, please. I've taken up too much of your time as it is."

"I'll walk you there myself, and I'll ask Kate to bring you a box for Jack's personal items. He has some pictures and a few desk items you'll probably like to have. I'll then have the carton packed up properly for shipping and sent to your house in Aspen. What are you going to do about his condo?"

"When we find out for sure what happened to him, and if our suspicions prove to be right, I'll come back to take care of it or let the attorney hire a management company to vacate and sell it. I'm sure the lawyer will have some suggestions as to what to do."

They rose and walked out of Michael's office and down the hall. As they approached Jack's office, Michael said, "Come back down when you're done. Don't leave without saying goodbye."

"Okay. And thanks. This won't take me long."

When Michael left Lauren, she sighed with relief. She needed some time to herself to process the information he had sprung on her. She walked into Jack's office and put her purse and raincoat on a guest chair. Jack occupied the opposite corner office, with an equally fantastic view and similar western-style decor. She sat down at the oak desk, which looked just like Michael's, and took a deep breath, her mind coming up with a number of different scenarios.

Why would Michael even suggest that Jack could be responsible for the death of an employee?

Trying to understand Michael's conclusion, she decided to follow his train of thought to see where it might lead. *Maybe Jack hadn't been sick at all right before he boarded the plane. He could have sabotaged the plane himself, knowing that he was responsible for Omar's ambush, and then planned to skip out. He may have thought that she, Lauren, had seen him after the plane took off and would be suspicious. Perhaps he was using her to help him escape, knowing that she'd been in love with him in college. Maybe he'd sent her to Houston to chase a red herring and distract Michael while he planned to escape his past, travel to some remote island, and live out the rest of his life in comfort. He'd even asked her not to tell her sister that he hadn't been on the plane.*

Stop now, she told herself. Her imagination was careening out of control. That sounded a bit too farfetched. *Was Michael Dodson even trustworthy? And why had the witness, Paul Johnson, arranged to meet me at the bar? Why did he walk out? Is he real? If he is real, Jack must be sincerely trying to solve things, and Michael's conclusions are wrong.*

Her heart told her to trust Jack. Taking a deep breath, she tackled the job at hand and started to put what looked to be his personal items in a segregated area to be boxed up and shipped to her home.

CHAPTER 18

Andy Harris, head of security and operations manager of Last Defense, lived close to the office in an apartment that fit his bachelor lifestyle. Not handsome in a Hollywood sense, he did have a clean-cut farm boy appearance, which hid the fact that he had been a Navy SEAL. With a congenial personality, he did well in the romance department and engaged in frequent love affairs, never settling down to the thought of marriage. He also required a low-maintenance home and life style so that he could accommodate his many trips out in the field.

Getting home late the previous night from a weeklong field assignment, he arrived later than usual at work. As he walked through the hallway, he noticed the door to Jack's office was open. Andy knew that Jack was missing, so he strode in to investigate. "Good morning," he said, his eyes finding Lauren.

"Good morning," Lauren replied, startled out of her thoughts as she placed a photograph on a pile of Jack's belongings.

"I'm Andy Harris, head of security here," the man said in a tone that suggested he wanted her to explain her presence. "Who are you?"

"I'm Lauren Reese, from Aspen, Colorado. I was a friend of

Jack's, and I came here to gather some of his personal things. I'm sure you've heard. The commuter plane that he was on from Aspen to Denver is missing—the control tower lost contact with it."

Andy stared at Lauren with a puzzled look on his face.

"Nice to meet you," Lauren said in a nervous tone as she held out her hand.

"Same here," Andy said, shaking her hand. His grip was incredibly strong, and she had to resist the urge to grimace.

He studied her with intent interest.

"You can understand my concern, since I'm responsible for our security," Andy said. Did Michael bring you in?"

"Yes, he did. I didn't breach security. I was invited in to pack up Jack's personal items."

Andy scanned the room. "Have you found anything interesting?"

"No, I'm not here to snoop around. I'm just here to pack up Jack's stuff."

"Okay, I see. I guess someone needs to do that."

"Have you ever been to Colorado?" Lauren asked in an attempt at small talk.

Andy nodded. "Denver and Colorado Springs. I've never been to Aspen, though. I've heard it's beautiful there."

"It is. It's a world-class ski resort. I'm sure you've heard of Aspen's reputation."

"Yes, of course. Don't a lot of movie stars ski there?"

"That's right. Playground for the rich and famous."

"How do you like Houston? Must be quite a change for you, huh?"

"Nice city, what I've seen of it through the rain." Lauren smiled.

Andy smiled, too, but then his expression turned serious.

"We all liked and respected Jack, and we are very sorry to hear about the plane. We hate to think the worst, but it doesn't look like Jack will be coming back. I often helped Jack with his planning and organizing, and it's going to be tough now to do it without him. We

all wear many hats here. I'm also involved in strategic operations."
All of a sudden he looked as if he was anxious to leave the room.
"Well, Lauren, I haven't even checked in with Michael yet, so I've
got to do that. Please excuse me and carry on with your packing. It
was nice to meet you."

"It was good to meet you, too . . ."

Before Lauren could finish her sentence, Andy had turned to
make his way down the hall.

Not a very friendly guy, Lauren thought. *It probably just threw him
off guard to find a stranger in the office with no advanced warning.* Still, she
wondered how often Andy traveled out in the field to work on site
to plan or help with operations. She made a mental note to try and
find out if he'd been in Afghanistan when Omar was ambushed.

She continued her search of Jack's desk for personal items to
pack, pleased she hadn't yet found any pictures of him with another
woman anywhere in his office. That would really have upset her.
It was unrealistic to think that Jack wasn't dating anyone, but she
hoped that he wasn't involved in a serious relationship at this time.
The only picture on his desk was one of him and his dad that had
been taken on a fishing trip. She put the photo on the stack to be
packed up.

Jack looked so happy in it. She remembered him telling her of
the fabulous excursions in Canada that he and Rick used to take.
Those were clearly better times, so it was no wonder Jack kept the
picture atop his desk to remind him of them. She also noticed a
painting of Aspen on his wall. *That must be his personal artwork.* She
took down the picture and studied it, recognizing the area. It made
her feel good to see that Jack also must have had fond memories
of Colorado.

Placing the painting aside, curiosity got the better of her. An
oak credenza set against the wall beckoned her. Noticing a stack of
unopened mail that looked like it had just been delivered recently,
she began thumbing through it. At the bottom of the stack she
found a manila envelope sent from a law firm in Houston. Hoping

that no one would mind, she opened it and pulled out a sheaf of documents.

Sitting down at Jack's desk again, she began to review the contents of the envelope. The top document contained a summary of the wrongful death suit, stating that the Kasim family was seeking $5 million in damages. The document looked like a copy, so she assumed that Michael had received the same set of papers.

Glancing at the round-faced Seth Thomas clock on the wall, she noticed that it was almost noon. She should try to contact Jack again, but she didn't think it would be a good idea to call from the Last Defense office. Anyway, she had already left him a message earlier telling him she wasn't coming home today.

She thought it imperative to try again to meet with Paul Johnson—her reason for coming to Houston in the first place. She checked her phone again in case she'd missed any calls or text messages. Nothing. Maybe Jack had heard from Paul.

More importantly, she was anxious to meet with Ali Kasim tomorrow. Ali had probably heard about the plane. Only in Houston could she help Jack, and besides, another plus about being here was that she was enjoying some much-needed time off from work.

She was just thinking she was feeling a bit hungry when, as if reading her mind, Michael appeared in the doorway.

"There are sandwiches and drinks in the conference room," he said with a smile. "We're all too busy to go out for lunch today so I had it brought in. I'm sorry, bad timing. We're working on an important proposal right now. As I told you, we're shifting our focus to other lines of business and trying to land a lucrative training contract."

"I am a little hungry," Lauren said. "Don't worry about entertaining me, though. Just pretend I'm not even here. I'm stacking Jack's personal items over there to be packed up."

"Feel free to ask me if you need anything else. Weren't you going home today? Do you need a ride to the airport?"

"Thanks, but I've decided to stay in Houston another day."

Instinct told her not to mention Ali and the letter she had found written to Jack.

"Good. Maybe I can spend more time with you, then."

Lauren followed Michael to the conference room to pick up her lunch. The sandwiches were marked, and she took a turkey and Swiss cheese on rye along with some chips. She found drinks in a small refrigerator. She pulled out a diet cola.

"Would it be all right if I ate in Jack's office?" she asked.

"Of course," Michael replied. "Perhaps I'll see you later."

She took the food with her back to Jack's office and sat down at his desk to eat. As she munched on the sandwich she became lost in thought.

So who is the traitor? Is it Jack? Michael? Who else would have been able to set up a double cross against Omar? And why? What did Omar know or do to cause someone to kill him?

She didn't like being suspicious of everyone. Especially Jack. Then she remembered what Omar had written—*it's hard to trust anyone.*

Part of her wished that she could go back to that first encounter with Jack at the airport and forget everything else that had happened since. But she couldn't go back in time. She could only move forward and try to find out the dark secrets hidden behind the walls of Last Defense.

Lauren stood up and placed her sandwich wrap in the trash can. *This is driving me crazy. Maybe I can get more information from Michael.*

Finding him alone in his office, she strode in purposefully and sat down in the same leather chair she'd sat in earlier.

"I'm going to get right to the point. Do you think it's possible that someone else at Last Defense, other than Jack, could have been responsible for the death of your employee?"

Once again, she was dismayed she'd taken such a direct approach with him. She'd have to be more careful with her words Hopefully, Michael would think that she was trying to protect Jack's reputation and his estate. But she could see by the look on his face that she had made a mistake by being so pointed. Hopefully, it was not a fatal one.

Michael looked like he was becoming concerned with Lauren and her questions. His facial expression and body language gave Lauren the message that he was losing patience.

"Honestly, I trust all our employees," he said. "Besides an extensive background check, we put all our candidates through an intense computer-generated screening process. It tests all potential employees for personality type and loyalty. The software engineer and recruitment manager, Joseph Chen, who is in charge of our program, is in his office. Would you like to meet him?" Michael looked like he was more than happy to show off their technology and end this conversation.

"Yes, I would, thanks." Lauren followed him to the end of another corridor, to an office significantly smaller than Michael's.

Joe Chen was a friendly, Asian man, mid to late twenties, with angular features and straight black hair. He wore glasses with designer frames and smiled as Michael introduced him to Lauren. He seemed excited to tell her all about the software he had helped develop for Last Defense, explaining to her that the computer software program was more advanced than a lie detector test because it was able to measure the qualifications, personality, honesty, and loyalty of all potential employees. Lauren was skeptical but tried to show interest. *How could a computer measure such things? Are these people serious?*

She tried to act as if she was completely taken in by this new technology as she listened to Joe's demonstration of the program's nuances. "This is very interesting stuff," she said. "Computers have really come a long way." *Soon we won't need people,* she thought.

"This software is state of the art. It measures physical and emotional responses to various suggestions and questions. We use it to screen all of our employees. It must work because our employees are the best. There has never been an incident."

Right, thought Lauren.

"You look skeptical. Would you like to try it yourself?"

"Sure. Why not?"

Joe had Lauren sit down while he placed a band around her upper arm and another one around each of her wrists, as if she were taking a lie detector test. He then asked her various questions. She answered each one naturally and matter-of-factly, although she was worried. Would her stress level indicate that she was deceiving people about Jack's "death" and the reason for her visit? Doing her best to stay calm, she smiled and Joe began the test.

"What is your name?" Joe asked.

"Lauren Reese."

"Why are you in Houston?"

Oh, boy, here we go. I'm going to fail this one.

"I'm here to help out a family friend."

That was something she could honestly say. Joe then asked her other general questions about what she did for a living, where she was from, and questions about the country, which she assumed would indicate how patriotic she was. Civics had been one of her favorite subjects in school, and she was thrilled that she could answer almost all the questions about the United States government, judicial system, and history correctly. The test lasted about half an hour. Joe said that he would analyze the results and report back to her sometime tomorrow. After the visit with him and watching a short film presentation that Joe had produced and directed about Last Defense, Lauren expressed her gratitude to him for spending time teaching her about the software he had developed.

"You are very innovative. Last Defense is lucky to have you," Lauren said as she prepared to leave. In truth, she was so happy the test was over, she would have said anything to get out of there.

"Thank you for your interest in our company," Joe replied.

Lauren then walked down the hall, and, finding Michael in his office, told him she was leaving for the day and thanked him for his hospitality. Andy was in the office as well, and the two men looked

105

like they were having an important discussion. Embarrassed that she'd interrupted them, she smiled at Andy to acknowledge his presence.

"Why don't you come back in tomorrow?" Michael suggested. I won't be as busy then and can spend more time with you. I can introduce you to our lawyers if you want. It would probably be good for you to meet them since talking to people over the phone becomes more personal after you've actually seen them."

"Thank you, Michael. I'd like that."

"It's settled, then. Are you heading back to the Hyatt now?"

"Yes, but I've booked another room. I appreciate the suite you provided for me, but perhaps one of your clients would like to use it?"

"You probably don't want any more surprise visitors, either, eh?" Michael chuckled. "Again, I apologize. I didn't intend for you to find me in the room."

"That's okay. That's not it. I just don't want to impose," Lauren said, concerned that by changing rooms she was giving him the impression that she didn't trust him.

Andy looked at them with a quizzical expression on his face, like he was being kept out of an inside joke. Glad to be leaving the office, Lauren just smiled and said goodbye.

She wanted to go back to her room, relax, and reflect on the events of the day. She also wanted to call Jack and tell him about the letter she'd found in his mailbox since she hadn't mentioned it in the message she'd left him earlier. Her gut feeling told her that the letter was very significant. Would Jack be open to her plan to reach out to Ali Kasim? Another reason she was anxious to talk to him was that she hoped he had heard something from Paul Johnson.

Lauren crossed the reception area and asked Kate to call a taxi for her.

"Sure. Leaving so soon? I hope we didn't scare you off."

"No, I'm going to run some errands and maybe do some

sightseeing," she said, lying to Kate to give her the impression that she was going to act like a typical tourist. "Everyone here has been very gracious."

Michael had apparently overheard her. He and Andy suddenly appeared in the lobby. "No need to call a taxi. Andy can give you a ride wherever you would like to go. He can show you the city if you're interested. I would do the honors myself but I have a client coming to meet with me within the hour."

Puzzled, Lauren debated what to do. How could she call Jack if she was with Andy? And why did Michael think she needed to be chaperoned? Was he being kind, or not willing to let her out of sight because she'd been asking too many questions? If she refused, would that make him even more suspicious? And would they follow her anyway, if keeping an eye on her was their intent?

"That is very kind. Sure. Andy can give me a lift if it is not too much trouble."

"I'm happy to give you a ride and show you the city," Andy responded. "I could use a break, myself, since I just got home last night."

They took the elevator down to the underground parking lot of the building. Andy drove a charcoal grey Lexus ES. A nice car and not as pretentious as what Michael drove.

He seemed happy to be getting out of the office and playing the role of taxi driver and tour guide. He opened the door for her and was quite the gentleman, much friendlier that when she'd first met him.

As she entered his car, her purse became tangled and the contents of it spilled onto the floor. Andy picked them all up for her and handed the errant objects over.

"Sorry about that," Lauren said as she settled into the passenger seat."

"No problem." Andy climbed in the driver's seat next to her. He had noticed the container of pepper spray. As he started the car and pulled out of the parking space, he asked, "Why do you carry pepper spray? Don't you feel safe? Or is it just to protect yourself from men in general?"

Lauren laughed. "I feel very safe. I'm with the head of security, remember?" Lauren smiled at Andy and then said in a serious tone, "It's just that I'm a stranger in a big city, a woman traveling alone."

Andy glanced at her. "It's always good to have protection. Can I give you some advice?"

"Please do."

"Don't get involved with Michael Dodson. He is recently divorced and looking for a rebound relationship. His divorce was hard on him."

"Thanks," Lauren said, wondering why Andy would say such a thing. Did Andy know about her date with Michael last night, or did he just assume that they'd gone out together from what Michael had said in his office? What had they been talking about, and how much of their conversation included her and her presence in Houston?

As Andy pulled out of the parking garage and headed toward the freeway, he asked in a cheerful tone, "Where would you like to go?"

"Well, if you're up for it, I wouldn't mind seeing some of the city. What do you recommend?"

"How'd you like me to take you to a quaint historic town on the coast? You look like you need to relax. I think you would like it."

"Fantastic and I really do need to relax," she replied. "Tell me more about Houston," she said, pretending to be on a typical vacation trip.

"Houston is the fourth largest city in the country," he told her proudly. "And we're also on top of the world because the first word spoken on the moon was Houston."

Lauren laughed. "So, tell me a little about its history. Wasn't Houston originally part of Mexico?"

"You do know your history lessons. Yes, it was originally part of the Spanish territories, which Mexico took over. But a lot of adventurous Americans settled in Texas, too. The population became a combination of Mexicans and Americans. That's why you'll hear the term "Tex Mex." The city began developing in the 1840s, and then became a part of something that could have been big. Did you know that Texas declared itself a Republic, and was seeking international recognition as an independent country?" Not waiting for an answer, he followed with, "But you know how things go."

"You mean that men are always fighting each other for what they want, whether it's theirs or not?" Lauren asked, laughing to herself. She used to admire Jack because he talked about how he would always fight for his beliefs. She wondered if that's what he thought he was doing now. Her thoughts digressed to Michael, who was a real fighter, a veteran of war.

Andy kept talking. "The city is named after Sam Houston, an American who defeated the Mexicans. Texas became a state in 1846." Then he changed his tone.

"What about you?" he asked with a conspiratorial grin. "What's going on? Looks like you know all about us now. You were a friend of Jack's, you've met Michael and you've taken an employee screening test with Joe Chen. It seems as though you know all the ins and outs of Last Defense. So, now it's your turn. Tell me about yourself."

"It's kind of a long story," Lauren said as she gazed out the window.

Just then her cell phone rang, and she pulled it out of her purse. The caller ID indicated it was Jack, so she turned her phone off and slid it back into her purse. She didn't want to talk to him in front of Andy for obvious reasons. The message tone sounded and curiosity got the best of her. She quickly opened her purse and glanced at the text on her phone.

WTF?!

Lauren wasn't surprised. She knew Jack would not approve of

her staying another day. As soon as she had an opportunity, she would call him and explain her decision.

"How well did you know Jack?" Andy inquired. "I never heard him mention you."

"He was my boyfriend in college. He wouldn't have mentioned me. We drifted apart but stayed friends. He would visit me when he came to Aspen for ski trips. He asked me to look after his dad if anything ever happened to him, and also to be the executor of his estate."

"I see. That's a lot to ask of a friend."

"Well, it wasn't just the two of us who knew each other. Our families were close and they had a long history."

"How much did Jack tell you about Last Defense?"

"Not much. He came to Aspen to ski and not talk shop."

"He must have told you about the lawsuit and the tragedy in Afghanistan involving one of our finest men."

"Yes, he did mention it. He wasn't forthcoming with many details, though. The main reason I came to Houston was to visit Jack's dad and try to determine care for him."

"We were sorry to hear about Jack's dad. Jack said the man has lost his memory and some physical abilities."

"I know. I went to visit him when I arrived on Monday night. I could tell he didn't remember me at all."

Driving on the busy network of interstate highways, Lauren was able to see many of the modern buildings that adorned the city. The rain had subsided and the sun was peeking out from under a cloud. Heading southeast, they arrived at their destination. Andy drove to a parking lot on the waterfront and parked the car.

She was glad for this sea change. It got her mind off of the serious aspects of her trip and let her be what she was pretending to be—a tourist.

"Would you like to walk around?" Andy asked.

"Yes. Love to."

Strolling along the crushed granite trail system with Andy,

Lauren finally began to shed some of the stress she'd built up from her morning revelations. Even though the air was a bit chilly, she was comfortable looking out at the harbor, the scene so different from her usual surroundings. The serenity of the port town soothed her soul. This could be her last day in Texas to sightsee, and she wanted to hold on to the moment. She took out her phone and snapped several pictures.

Lauren struck up a conversation with Andy as they walked, "Why did you get involved with Last Defense?" she asked.

"Like many of our employees, I had just left the military. I'd been a Navy SEAL and wasn't able to adjust well to civilian life. I found myself still looking for action and not ready to settle down, so when I was introduced to Mike Dodson I immediately respected him and his company. It seemed like a great career move. I haven't been sorry."

"You were a Navy SEAL?"

He nodded. "I know that surprises people because of my boyish good looks," he said with a grin.

"I wasn't surprised at all. I just meant that I don't meet a Navy SEAL every day. I'm humbled, and appreciate that you are taking the time to be my tour guide."

"It is my pleasure. Like I said, I just got back in from the field so I needed the break, too."

"Since you gave me advice on my love life, how about you? Are you seeing anyone?"

"I am seeing someone right now."

"Is it serious?"

"Not serious. It's more of a casual fling. I'm not ready to settle down yet."

By his last comment, and the look on his face, Lauren wondered if it was Andy or his girlfriend that was making the decision about the seriousness of the relationship. She changed the subject.

"Getting back to Last Defense. Who are the main clients of the company?" Lauren asked.

"The Defense Department, the U.S. Agency for International Development, the State Department, and several private corporations. Many of our employees also act as bodyguards for U.S. generals and diplomats. Never a dull moment."

"I guess not. It sounds very exciting."

"Tell me more about you. What do you do?"

Lauren laughed, "My job is boring in comparison to yours. Are you sure you want to hear about it?"

"What seems boring to you might not be boring to me at all. I guess in time any job becomes . . . just a job."

"That's true. Once you've mastered your craft, the challenge is gone and the job becomes routine."

Andy shook his head. "Working in Aspen can't be boring, Lauren. Most people would be star struck, what with all the celebrities walking around, not to mention royalty from Europe and the Middle East. Doesn't a Saudi prince live in Aspen?"

"Yes, I believe so."

"That must be exciting, too."

"You get used to the people and eventually don't even think about it," Lauren said. "If you did, you couldn't work there and do your job very well. Everyone needs a break and a vacation. You have to respect their privacy and treat them like any other customer. That's what most of them want."

Lauren told him about her job at the airport and about her home. They walked together for a while in silence while she took in the sights. Far in the distance, she made out a ship and watched as it disappeared from view. Resuming her steps, she closed her mind to any outside thoughts and concentrated on what she was seeing and hearing in the small seaport town.

They eventually found an area crowded with local shops and browsed along the storefronts to see what was for sale. She purchased a few souvenirs and enjoyed looking at the unique jewelry and clothing on display. When they walked past a small café, they went in and ordered coffee and a pastry to share. It was the break she needed to collect her thoughts before going back to Houston and calling Jack.

She would tell Jack about the letter but not about the conversation with Michael Dodson where he'd implicated Jack. How would she talk to Jack without letting it slip that she had been subjected to suspicion and innuendo about him? That she, herself, had begun to question his story?

After the casual and relaxing tour, she asked Andy to take her back to the Hyatt. She felt comfortable that he was convinced she was there as a tourist and to collect Jack's personal items, nothing more. With many thoughts running through her head, it didn't seem to take long before they arrived back at the hotel. Thanking him, she got out of the car.

Back in her new smaller room, this one bare of military artwork and magazines, she sat on the couch, took a deep breath, and reached in her purse for her cell phone and the letter from Ali Kasim. Punching in Jack's number, she was happy to hear his voice when he answered this time.

"Jack, before you say anything, let me explain."

"Explain," Jack said curtly.

"When I picked up your mail, there was a letter from Ali Kasim. Let me read it to you."

Jack seemed astonished when he heard the contents of the letter and about the letters that Omar had sent home.

"Omar had never mentioned any talk about illegal activity. I thought we were close enough that something like that would have been brought to my attention. I wonder what Omar learned that put him in danger." Jack said.

"So you understand why I wanted to stay another day. I want to talk to Ali Kasim. I called and talked to his daughter. She said he was out of town but will be back tomorrow."

"No, absolutely not!"

Lauren calmly said, "Okay, don't get excited."

"Promise me you will not contact Ali Kasim. I'll take it from here. I'll call Ali. You come home. Can't you see that you're in danger? I know I'm going to regret asking, but what have had you been doing all day?"

In pleasant tones she told him that, against his advice, she went to Last Defense. She described what happened during her day, talking nonstop so he didn't have a chance to say anything. She told him about the software demonstration, film presentation and tour, then explained that there had been no time to call him because she'd been in the company of Last Defense personnel all day.

"So where are you now? I thought we had an agreement that you were coming home today."

"I'm still at the Hyatt. How about Paul? Have you heard from him? I really did want to talk to him. It's too late for me to make a flight to Denver and then connect on to Aspen. I'll make the plane reservations right now for tomorrow, as soon as I get off the phone with you."

"Well, I guess I have no choice in this. Sounds like you've made up your mind. Okay, I guess I really can't stop you, can I?"

"No, I guess not. So, you haven't heard anything from Paul Johnson?"

"No."

"I just don't understand. I have sent him numerous text messages. It seems like he doesn't trust me, and I can't figure out why that would be."

"I don't know. It might be best if you don't send him any more text messages. He has probably just decided to not come forward with the information he said he had. Maybe he thought everything over and decided he was wrong, or maybe he just changed his mind. It happens."

"I was hoping I would still get a chance to meet with him before leaving and find out why he ditched our last meeting. I'm sure that I saw him."

"I don't have any idea why that happened. Just be safe and plan on leaving tomorrow. In the meantime, maybe you could do some more sightseeing. I really think you've done all you can to help me and I thank you, but it's time for you to come home, Lauren."

After saying goodbye and hanging up the phone, she felt a bit confused. Why did Jack sound like he wasn't telling her everything? He sounded evasive about Paul. Ultimately, she had no real reason to further her stay in Houston if she couldn't meet with Paul or Ali. As promised, she called the airline and booked a flight back to Colorado for the following afternoon.

Now she had more time to kill. *The life of a private investigator must be somewhat boring. Not glamorous like I always believed.* Luckily, another HBO movie that she had wanted to see was showing on the television in her room. Comfortably situated on the bed in front of the TV, she watched the movie.

When it was over, she wandered down to the hotel restaurant. There she treated herself to a glass of wine and a light dinner before returning to her room. *I have to call Shannon. I hope she's home so that I can share my experiences with her and maybe get some big sister advice. She's probably worried about me.*

"Hi, it's good to hear your voice. I was afraid you weren't home," Lauren said, relieved that her sister answered the phone after several rings.

"It's good to hear from you, too. I was just getting the kids out of the tub," Shannon said. Lauren pictured her sister holding the phone to her ear with her shoulder as she dried off her daughter. "How are things going in Houston?"

"Well, I'm seeing two men now," Lauren offered teasingly and was pleased when Shannon expressed surprise. "I went out to dinner last night with Jack's business partner, a man named Michael Dodson. He's former military, and he's very charming."

"You sound like you're in safe hands at least. However, I wonder what Jack would think about your date last night. I hope you didn't forget that he's waiting for you at our house."

"I know. It's just crazy. I don't know who I can trust. The plane is still missing and it doesn't look good. I don't think Jack was responsible, but it's possible he is, I guess. It could be Michael, too. They both seem to be implicating each other. In any case, I'm here in the middle of it."

"You think Jack might be responsible? That doesn't sound like the Jack I knew," Shannon said. "Lauren, I'm worried about you. You seem confused, and that isn't like you. You're always so grounded and decisive. Look, I don't know Jack very well, but I pride myself on reading people. What I remember about him when the two of you were dating was that he was an honorable, honest man who cared about you very much."

"I appreciate what you're saying, Shannon, and I'll give it lots of thought."

"That's all I can ask, I suppose," Shannon said.

"It's all right. I'm going to do a little more research, maybe go back to Jack's office, and then I'll be flying back in the afternoon. The witness that I was supposed to meet never showed up."

"The witness didn't show up? Call me as soon as you get back to Aspen. I want to hear about everything. In the meantime, be careful. I don't like the sound of what's going on there. Missing witnesses, charming and seductive business partners—sounds like something from a spy novel. Everyone seems a little too friendly. I'm worried about you."

"Oh, don't worry. I'll call you tomorrow as soon as I'm home. Speaking of home, you need to haul your family up to Aspen to take advantage of the great ski conditions."

"I know. We're planning a trip."

"Okay, I'll see you soon then. I love you."

"I love you, too."

Since there was no one else to talk to, she decided to turn in for the evening, slightly disappointed that Michael hadn't called. Why hadn't he called? Why did she care? Taking off her clothes and putting on her nightgown, she wished Jack were here with her. But Michael was acting like he was very interested in her as well. Who would believe? From zero to two men in four days!

Turning on the television in the bedroom to distract her thoughts, she could only handle about fifteen minutes of local news when she felt her eyes closing. She turned out the light, feeling somewhat secure. If Michael or anyone else tried to come through her door, she was ready, the pepper spray resting on the small table by the bed.

CHAPTER 19

A single man and a computer programmer, Joseph Chen not only used his computer to screen employees at work he also used it to screen his dates, and did so without permission or the knowledge of anyone at Last Defense.

He'd been in a relationship that ended badly years ago when he was deployed to Iraq and then to Afghanistan. His lengthy absences would have been hard on any relationship, but his computer program had explained the breakup much more to his satisfaction because it took into account factors of personality and IQ compatibility.

He believed a software program would help him find the perfect mate, and so far, none of his female companions passed the qualifications for a suitable girlfriend or wife. This was the computer age. The twenty-first century. No longer should people take seriously the notion of a chance romance, or, even worse, the arranged marriages like those still going on in India and other parts of the world.

He'd disregarded his last girlfriend's objections as female sentiment when she found out that the computer program hadn't deemed her suitable for him. He tried to forget his last personal conversation with her, but found it hard since they both worked together at Last Defense. An intelligent and educated woman, Kate Myers was baffled that Joe was making a strange and curious life decision based on arbitrary computer program results.

Since the moment that he had summoned her to his house to talk, she'd known something was up. On the drive toward his brick ranch, two-bedroom sparsely furnished home, she had a bad feeling about what the talk was going to be about. He had become distant in the last few weeks.

"Joe," she said. "How could the computer application know if a woman will stand by you if you come down with a major illness or financial setback? Is it really necessary that your partner have exactly the same interests as you? What if you played tennis and she didn't but was willing to go to the court to watch you and cheer you on? No one is perfect. We accept the flaws of the people we love, our family, our friends, and our mates. This is part of being human, and we are complex beings with many layers. You think your computer program gets into the hearts and minds of people, but it doesn't. Love, caring, and understanding come into play when other things let us down. People have the capability to surprise us. Computers don't."

While she talked, she suddenly realized she wasn't being heard. Joe had tuned her out. She accidently said the "L" word, which surely brought up his defensive shields. She did her best to get him to understand her point of view, but he just looked at her with a blank stare.

"I wish you well," she said as she threw down the set of house keys that he had given to her. "The voice on your smart phone or GPS won't talk you down off a ledge. There's not an app for that."

These were her final words as she walked out the door.

"Kate . . ."

It was too late. She was gone.

Driving home, Kate admonished herself for breaking one of her own cardinal rules—dating someone she worked with. Now she had to see Joe Chen every day while she pulled herself together from a heartbreaking and ridiculous rejection.

Growing up in a rough neighborhood in Los Angeles, the culturally traditional world of Joe's mother and father was shattered by the violence and crime they encountered as they tried to make a living in a hostile environment. Joe's older brother joined an Asian gang and was lost to it forever. But, Joe was determined to make his parents proud. He'd joined the Marines right after high school, and was now very successful in his professional life. Brilliant and educated, he'd found his niche working at Last Defense. Michael and Jack gave him the opportunities that he'd always longed for, and now he found himself a major partner in a highly successful company.

His computer software programs were working, given that the employees of Last Defense were never in trouble, and everyone recognized that they were the finest private security contractors in the industry. He finally could explain the world around him, or so he thought.

CHAPTER 20

fghanistan, six months earlier

A Land Cruiser carrying two private security contractors rolled down the Afghanistan highway to their next destination, an area near the Pakistani border, in Badakhshan province, a place generally unsafe for Americans. It was searingly hot and dusty, the landscape barren and hostile to living creatures. The driver had cranked up the air conditioner full blast. As the car approached what looked like an outpost, it slowed down and then stopped.

Omar sat in the passenger seat, silent, wishing he could be invisible. He felt like he was under constant pressure and that someone was watching him all the time. He never felt safe, especially when in a vehicle. The only time he felt safe was when he was in his hotel room with the deadbolt secured. He was getting tired of delays, secrets, lies, and endless directives from his bosses at Last Defense. He was forced to trust people he didn't know, he was never in control, and he had to do exactly as he was told. The money was good, but he'd finally reached his breaking point. This would be his last mission—once completed, he planned to quit his job and go home to Houston and be with his family.

An Afghani guard stood in the middle of the road with a

battered AK rifle hanging from his shoulder. As the driver rolled down the window, a wave of hot air entered the air-conditioned cabin of the Land Cruiser. He handed the guard some wrinkled paperwork—the manifest and the operating license of Last Defense. The process of moving around the country had become a constantly changing exercise in bureaucracy, fees, and bribery. But after a few minutes the guard waved them through.

A short time later, another convoy of contractors traveled along the same hot and dusty road. The driver in the first vehicle of the convoy noticed the Land Cruiser off to the side of the road and got out to investigate. When he looked closer he saw the Land Cruiser had a single bullet hole in the rear window. Then he saw a man in the passenger seat slumped over. He could see that the driver of the Land Cruiser was clearly shaken but unharmed. Opening the passenger door, he looked at the man spattered in blood and recognized Omar Kasim, a contractor he knew well. The driver, also a seasoned soldier, was confused and astonished at what he saw. The shot looked like it had come from a military sharpshooter sniper rifle, rather than an insurgent weapon. Why Omar Kasim?

On the outskirts of a military compound, a Humvee moved slowly down the road that cut through the poppy fields in a remote area of Afghanistan. Michael Dodson pulled up to the tallest building for his meeting with Colonel Shore, a well decorated Army officer. Michael had on a khaki uniform with a patch identifying him as an executive with Last Defense. Shore had a tanned, rough-looking face from years of chain smoking and four decades of military service, including Special Operations.

Colonel Shore offered Michael a cigar, which he declined. Another man entered Colonel Shore's office, wearing a khaki uniform similar to the one Michael had on, with a patch identifying him as a company field commander for another private security company. He introduced himself to Michael and Colonel Shore as

Mark Kemp. He accepted a cigar and sat down on one of the metal chairs in the room across from the Colonel. Shore and Kemp lit their cigars.

"What are you guys drinking? Is scotch okay?" Colonel Shore asked as he filled two glasses halfway with straight scotch, not waiting for an answer. Both gentlemen accepted their drinks, and Shore poured himself one as well. Kemp had been in the military and became offensive whenever Colonel Shore referred to his men as mercenaries.

"We are private security contractors," Mark said. "Everyone works for a living; everyone gets paid. If getting paid for your work makes you a mercenary, then everybody is a mercenary in one way or another."

"Point taken. I didn't mean to offend," said Shore. "Let's get down to business."

"I'm all for that. We're each here for the same purpose," Michael Dodson said as he sat down in another rusty metal chair.

"I'm concerned that the General will find out," Shore said. "This could ruin my career, if not put me in jail. But if we can pull this off, it will be big." He puffed on his cigar. "We've got to make sure no one finds out about this. We need to use only our most trusted men, ones who can keep a secret to their death."

"Last Defense doesn't usually get involved in this type of operation. How are the opiates being smuggled out of the country?" Michael inquired.

"That's the rub. An Iranian general is allowing Afghan narcotics traffickers to smuggle drugs through Iran."

"Geez, I guess everyone wants in on the action," said Mr. Kemp.

"You would be surprised how many people are in on this. Probably a majority of the locals have some association with the drug trade."

Michael Dodson put down his drink, got up, and walked over to the window. As he looked at the field before him, he said, "Just tell me what you want me to do."

CHAPTER 21

Thursday morning, after sleeping in until eight o'clock, Lauren woke up refreshed and ready for the day. She dressed in casual clothes, blue jeans and a white knit top, since her only goal today would be filling a few boxes to continue her ruse of packing Jack's personal belongings and traveling home.

Her pepper spray fit nicely in the back pocket of her jeans. Immediately she felt safer and ready to take on the day, as she looked forward to ending her mission in Houston and returning to her home in Aspen.

Getting a latte and a pastry to go at the café, she took a taxi to Last Defense. During the drive she was able to view her surroundings clearly, as the rain hadn't returned and the sun was again peeking out from the clouds. Houston's overall temperature was more moderate than Aspen's in winter.

It's probably twenty degrees at my house today, she thought. *This city does have some potential, now that it's stopped raining.*

Again, she asked the security guard to let Michael know she'd arrived. Kate came down to escort her up to the office lobby which appeared busy, with people bustling in and out.

She waited there for almost fifteen minutes before Michael came out to greet her. He invited her into his office and they both sat down—he at his desk and she in the comfortable leather guest chair.

"How are you today?" Michael said in an upbeat tone. He looked directly at her eyes, as if trying to judge her feelings.

"Fine, thanks," she said, not returning his look. "How about you?"

"Very well, thanks. Did you miss me last night? I'm sorry I couldn't spend the evening with you, but I had to take a client to dinner. As I told you, I've been trying to land a lucrative contract I've been working on for months. I was disappointed I couldn't get away."

She responded, "That's perfectly fine because I was exhausted and just watched TV before going to bed early. It must be this lower altitude." She giggled a little and added, "I guess, compared to Aspen, there is too much oxygen down here for me."

Michael got the joke and laughed, which was something she had rarely seen from this serious man. How great to see him smile. It made her think he could be a "regular" guy.

He said, "Well, it's nice to see you here again today. How about lunch later on?"

"Sure, sounds good, but it will have to be an early one. Maybe a brunch if that works for you. I'm just going to pack up a few more things of Jack's. I'll be leaving for Colorado on a three o'clock flight and would like to get to the airport early. I didn't want to lug my suitcase around today, so I asked for a delayed checkout at the hotel. You're right, Michael. They are very accommodating, maybe because they know I'm involved with Last Defense. Nonetheless they have been more than helpful."

"I'm glad that you stayed there. What a coincidence you picked the Hyatt to stay at, eh?"

Why did he say that? What is he getting at?

"I'll need to stop by the hotel and get my things. Maybe you could give me a ride?"

"Sure. I'm not as busy today as I was yesterday. My schedule is pretty clear. I only have one meeting later this afternoon, so why don't we spend the morning together? Just let me wrap a few things up first and we'll be off. Did you want to meet our lawyers? I can call them and arrange it if you would like."

"No, I think I'll pass on that. I'd love to spend more time with you before I leave, though. By the way, how did your meetings go yesterday? Did you get the contract?"

"Yes, we did. They called me this morning with the news. You can help me celebrate."

"Congratulations. I would love to help you celebrate. By the way, you look more relaxed today. It's good to see you less formal and more like…."

"A regular guy?" Michael finished her sentence.

"Yeah, I guess that's what I mean," Lauren said as she smiled with the happy confidence of knowing they were both now acting like friends.

He was dressed in casual pants and shirt, and Kate was also dressed more casually, which indicated that the client they were trying to impress would not be in the office today. Lauren didn't feel out of place because she had on jeans, something she'd been worried about earlier.

"You know where Jack's office is, so go ahead and let yourself in. Kate put some boxes in the room for you. I'll come get you soon."

"Were you still going to arrange to have the boxes I'm packing shipped to my house in Aspen like we talked about earlier?"

"Yes. Or maybe I could bring them to you personally."

Lauren blushed. Again, he was flirting with her, and she feared that she would fall under his charming spell.

"I'm truly sorry," he said, "that you're leaving so soon. I would love to see you again under different circumstances. Get to know you better."

"I'm sure we can arrange that," she said, flashing him a beautiful smile.

"By the way, Lauren, people are starting to speculate and are asking if there is going to be a memorial service for Jack of some kind. If so, will it be here in Houston?"

"First of all, we don't know for certain that Jack is dead. If he is, I'd need some time to think about a service, but I'll let you know. I suppose it should be held in Houston, so I would come back, of course."

Lauren walked down the hall to Jack's office. As she entered the room, she noticed someone had been there and had gone through his papers. She glanced around the room, wondering if anything had been taken. Had she missed something yesterday?

Startled by a knock on the door, she looked up to see Joe Chen standing in the doorway.

"Do you mind if I have a word with you?" he said as he entered the office.

"Of course not, Joe. What is it?"

"I'm now performing the CFO duties until we can find a replacement for Jack. Not that he would be easy to replace. He was a great guy."

"So, you're assuming that Jack has met an untimely end?" she asked.

"I know Jack. He would have called by now if he was alive. If he was hurt seriously, burned over half of his body, he would still find a way to get in touch with us. That was Jack."

"I think you're right. He was like that. So you have another job on your plate now. You must be very busy with all you have to do, and now this."

"That isn't all. I found out this morning that our controller quit with no notice. He just walked out, so I have to hire someone to replace him, too. It's been one of those weeks. I really don't know where to start."

"Why did your controller quit?"

"He got another job, I guess. That was what he said, anyway. I didn't think he was the type of person to walk out and not give two weeks' notice though. I'm baffled."

"Who was he?"

"His name is Ken Jones. I always thought he was doing a good job. Maybe he was upset about Jack. I think they were good friends and worked well together."

"Well, that happens. People get other offers or just decide that a job isn't right for them anymore. I'm sure it's not the best time for you, though. Now you have even more work to do. What are you working on right now?"

Lauren wondered why Joe was being so talkative and friendly. What were his motives? She supposed she should continue being friendly to him. If she did, maybe she would learn something new about the company or Jack's situation.

"I am trying to sort through some of the documents regarding the lawsuit," Joe said. "Did you run across anything here in Jack's office while you were sorting through everything yesterday?"

"Actually, I did. Over there by the window are some papers from the lawyers you'll probably need to see. But they're copies, so you might already have them."

There was no point in Lauren pretending she hadn't seen them. It could be a test to see if she were hiding anything.

"Okay, thanks," Joe said. He gathered the papers and then turned to face Lauren as he spoke. "One more thing, Lauren. The company lawyers have requested that I see your power of attorney document. Do you have it with you?"

"I'm sorry, Joe, I don't. I left it in my hotel room."

Lauren hoped Joe couldn't tell that she was lying. His suggestion that she wasn't to be completely trusted made her feel uncomfortable and he looked at her with suspicious eyes.

"Anything else, Joe?" Lauren asked.

"I was just wondering—Jack never mentioned you—I was wondering why he didn't." *Why do all these guys say that? Is this company one big locker room where they all discuss their sexual escapades and personal relationships?*

She again explained her relationship with Jack and his family to Joe.

"Did Michael allow you to come in on your own?" Joe asked suddenly. "He is so trusting, especially when an attractive woman is involved. The man thinks with his dick."

Joe realized what he'd just said and to whom. He became embarrassed and apologetic. "I'm sorry. I shouldn't have said that. I'm used to being around men. That was very inappropriate of me to say. I'm just trying to follow protocol and the instructions from the lawyers."

Joe's language didn't bother Lauren. She realized the company had a male culture. She actually thought Joe had been very polite, considering all that he was going through.

"Michael has allowed me to pack Jack's office by myself. He doesn't think that there is anything to hide. He's certain Last Defense didn't do anything wrong," Lauren said.

"I hope he's right."

"I hope he is, too."

"Great. So if you find anything else that may be helpful to me as I transition into Jack's job, please bring it to my office. And when you talk to Jack's lawyer, make sure you mention that Jack's estate might be included in the lawsuit and/or the criminal investigation. He should be made aware of everything and should contact our lawyers as soon as possible."

"I'll be sure to mention that," Lauren said, and then she became daring. "Why do you think that Jack was becoming suspicious of what was going on in Afghanistan?"

"He didn't tell me too much, but I know that the Defense Department called and had questions about several invoices we had sent them. We'd billed them for security services rendered in a few areas that we weren't authorized to be in."

"What did Michael say about these unauthorized areas?"

"He said that some of these bureaucracies are so big that the left hand doesn't know what the right hand is doing. In other words, the person on the end of the phone might not think we were authorized to be there, but that doesn't mean that someone else in the organization didn't request our being there for some other reason and didn't feel the need to communicate it with anyone else."

"That makes sense. I'm sure he's right about that." Again, Lauren wondered why Joe was being so friendly and open with her. Did he just need to talk to someone?

"I do know that one of the areas that the Defense Department questioned was Omar's location before he was transferred. Omar got very defensive and upset when Jack questioned him about being there. Then he was transferred to where he was ambushed."

The implication of Joe's last sentence stung Lauren.

"Did that happen often? I mean, the Defense Department questioning invoices?"

"I don't think so, but Ken, the controller that just quit, would be the one that would know more about that. He was working with Jack on getting the invoices approved and paid, which they were eventually."

"Would you have Ken's phone number? I would like to talk to him."

"I'll see if I can find it. What did Jack tell you about all of this?" Joe asked.

Lauren feigned ignorance. "He didn't tell me anything about it. I was just wondering as a result of what I've heard since I've been here. But don't worry. I know it's none of my business, and I'll be out of here soon. I don't want to get in your way or make your job more difficult. Jack's lawyer might want Ken's number, that's all. Right now, I'm waiting for Michael. We're going to spend the morning together and then he's going to drive me to the airport."

What with Joe's previous comment about Michael's priorities and by the look on his face, Lauren could guess what Joe was thinking.

"He is? Well, just show Michael the Power of Attorney then.

That will make the lawyers happy."

"Okay, I'll show it to him. By the way, how did I do on your pre-employment test yesterday?"

"Good. You're hired. When can you start?"

His serious face broke in to a smile that made Lauren feel more at ease. He couldn't very well still be suspicious of her when the computer software program he was so proud of had indicated she was employable. Lauren knew how to get on his good side, and she'd found his weak spot, his pride.

"If I don't get back to Aspen soon, I may be in the market for a new job, so I might have to take you up on your offer," Lauren said with a laugh, feeling more at ease and comfortable to be there.

"You can be our new controller," Joe joked.

"I don't have an accounting degree."

"That's okay. Neither did Ken."

Both laughed and then Joe said, "Just kidding. I don't know what Ken's credentials were. He was hired because Jack was dating his aunt, and that's all I knew about him."

This new information raised a red flag for Lauren. "I hope things calm down for you," she said.

"Calm down? Never. But I'll be getting the help I need soon. Our CPA firm is sending candidates for both positions tomorrow. They think they'll each be a good fit."

"I'm glad to hear that. Well, it's been a pleasure to meet you, Joe. I loved watching your film."

"Thanks. I guess all my hard work has paid off. It looks like we just got a lucrative contract."

"Congratulations."

"Thanks. We could really use Jack now."

"You wouldn't be in the position you are in if you couldn't handle the new challenge."

"I guess you're right. Well, goodbye, Lauren. Have a safe trip back to Colorado."

Joe left, and despite his pleasant manner, Lauren was starting to feel like she had worn out her welcome. She'd also gotten the impression that Joe had no intention of giving her Ken Jones's phone number. Maybe she could get it from Kate. She made a mental note to ask for it.

No sooner had Joe left, and Michael entered Jack's office, looking serious and slightly bewildered, so much different than his earlier demeanor.

"Lauren, could you follow me to my office, please?" he said. "I've got an important visitor I want you to meet."

Lauren could sense that this was not a good thing. Wondering who it could possibly be, she quickly followed Michael, trailing two steps behind him.

In his office waited a man wearing a dark suit, with a rather somber look on his face. He offered Lauren a business card.

"My name is James Stafford. I'm with the FBI."

Lauren took his card and stood in disbelief. She realized that she was in serious trouble and should not have stayed another day. *Why didn't I listen to Jack and take the first plane out of here yesterday?*

"Yes, sir, how can I help you?" she said, struggling to keep her voice steady.

"I am involved in the investigation of the missing plane out of Aspen."

"I see. Have they found the plane?"

"Yes, the investigators have found it. They've determined the plane was sabotaged with a small explosive device set to go off at a certain altitude. It didn't completely demolish the plane, but the explosion was enough to bring it crashing down. There are no survivors."

Lauren felt her heartbeat accelerate in her chest.

"I guess our fears have been realized," she said in a shaky voice.

"Our investigation has also revealed that Jack Kelly was not on the plane."

Lauren could feel Michael's stare even before she looked over at him. Her face turned warm as she feigned surprise.

"Really? I don't understand," Lauren said.

"Do you have any speculations about why Jack Kelly was not on the plane?" Agent Stafford asked.

"No. I haven't heard from Jack since the plane left the Aspen airport, but I did see him earlier in the week. He told me that if anything happened to him, he would like me to be the executor of his estate. He had no family other than his father who's in an assisted living facility, suffering from dementia and unable to take care of himself."

She hated to tell lies, but under the circumstances, she felt she had no choice. It was best to stick to the same story she had been telling everyone—she was the executor of Jack's estate and that she'd come to Houston mainly to check on his dad. She didn't know whom she could trust and was taken by surprise at the arrival of the FBI.

"Did he think he was in danger?" inquired Agent Stafford. "Did he have any reason to suspect that someone was trying to kill him?"

"I don't know. Our families were close, and he might have just reached out to me, considering his dad's condition. I believe his asking me to take care of his affairs was something he had wanted to do for a long time and just hadn't had the opportunity. He hadn't been to Aspen since his father became ill, as far as I know, and probably had it on his agenda to talk to me about these things."

Michael and Agent Stafford looked at each other as if they were sharing a secret or suspicions.

"Where are you staying?" Agent Stafford inquired.

"I'm at the Hyatt, but I'm leaving to go back to Aspen this afternoon. I just came to Houston to check on Jack's father and see if I could be of any help in case Jack truly had perished in an airplane crash. I'm shocked and don't know what to say. Where could Jack be?"

"We were hoping you could tell us," Agent Stafford said.

"I have no idea," Lauren replied.

As she spoke, Michael glared at her with surprise and suspicion. Her heart jumped in her throat as she realized that she could now be in imminent danger. If Michael suspected she had been in touch with Jack, she had to leave this situation immediately.

"Please contact me if you can think of anything else you can remember Jack telling you. Also, let me know immediately if you hear from Jack Kelly. We're working with the National Transportation and Safety Board to investigate who could have sabotaged the plane and why. We'll probably need to contact you again, so could you give me your cell number and your address in Aspen?"

"Yes, of course."

Michael handed her a pen and a pad of paper. Lauren wrote down her information and handed it to Agent Stafford.

The agent left, and Lauren immediately excused herself to visit the ladies room and call Jack on her cell phone.

With shaking hands, Lauren called Jack. He answered right away, to her relief.

"Jack, the FBI was here at the office—here at Last Defense." In short breaths she told him about their visit, what the agent said about the explosive device, and that they knew he wasn't on the plane.

"This is getting out of hand," Jack told her. "I insist that you immediately take a taxi to the airport and get on the first plane back to Colorado. I didn't want you to be caught up in this mess."

"I'm on my way, Jack," Lauren assured him.

"Good. I'll contact the FBI and explain everything to them. Most of all, I just want you to be safe."

"You're right," she responded. "I'll get on the first flight leaving for Denver. I'll call you as soon as I get to the gate so that at least you'll know I'm on my way."

"Okay, then. I'll wait for your call."

As Lauren walked out of the ladies room, Michael immediately accosted her from behind. Clearly, he'd been waiting outside the door for her. Grabbing her wrist, he turned her around, pinning her up against the wall, and pried the cell phone out of her hand. His strength frightened her, reminding her of who and what she was dealing with. She wouldn't be a match for him physically if he meant to hurt her, or, for that matter, if he wanted to get information from her.

"I know you were just talking to someone. Who did you call?" he demanded. "Was it Jack? Did you just lie to the FBI?"

Lauren struggled to regain her composure and catch her breath. She was tired of telling lies. She looked him straight in the eye.

"Yes, I called Jack."

CHAPTER 22

Michael studied the cell phone he had taken from Lauren. Pressing some buttons, he tried to find Jack's number. "Where is he?" he demanded.

Lauren didn't want to tell him that Jack was staying at her house. She didn't trust him—and still wondered if Michael had tried to kill Jack. At this point she wasn't sure if she trusted Jack, either. "I don't know," she responded as calmly as she could. "I called him on his cell phone. I don't know where he is."

"Either you're his partner or he's using you for his own ends. Which is it?" Michael put a firm hand on her arm so that she couldn't walk away.

She had no choice but to tell him at least part of the truth. "I saw Jack at the airport on Saturday. I hadn't seen him in years. We hadn't stayed in touch. Later Saturday night I heard about the missing plane on the television news. Jack contacted me and said that he never got on the plane, and that he thought someone had tried to kill him. I believed him. I came here to try to find out who would have a motive to kill him."

Trying to compose herself, she took a deep breath and loosened herself from Michael's grip. Just then, a woman walked by, headed toward a different office.

Quickly, Michael said, with no trace of warmth in his voice, "Let's go into my office. We need to talk."

Kate glanced up from her desk with surprise at Michael and Lauren as they walked into his office. By the look on her face, clearly she could tell they were not having a pleasant encounter. Agent Stafford had probably announced himself to Kate as an FBI agent, so most likely she was curious as to what was going on now between Michael and Lauren. Well, Lauren thought, *confidentiality is a major part of her job and critical to the company she works for. Whatever Kate was thinking, she'd keep it to herself.*

Inside Michael's office, Lauren sat down on the leather chair, which no longer seemed as comfortable as it had yesterday. Michael closed the door and then sat at his desk, deep in thought. He looked at Lauren.

"What if Jack planted that bomb?" Michael said tersely. "To fake his own death and escape his problems. He could be using you to gain information. Then he could remove you, too, and get away without taking responsibility for his actions." And then he added, "I'll have Joe track where he is by using the cell number that is stored in your phone. He also has a friend that works at the phone company."

In a panic, Lauren realized that it was just a matter of time before Michael found out that Jack was in Aspen.

"You think Jack did this?" she demanded, her voice a bit higher pitched than she would like.

"You think he would plant a bomb on a plane that would kill innocent people? Why would he do that?"

"Desperate people do desperate things." After these harsh words, Michael's face became more relaxed as he pondered what he had just said. He rubbed his face with his hands. Changing his tone, he said in an exasperated voice, "Look, I really don't know if Jack would do that. But someone obviously did. And Jack is sure looking guilty. He pretended to be on that flight. Haven't you wondered why he wasn't on the plane?"

"He explained that. He said he had a panic attack. He hadn't eaten all day, and he did look tired and stressed when I saw him at the airport before the plane took off."

"Do you really believe that?"

"I don't know what to believe or whom to trust."

"I want you to stay with me," Michael said in a calm voice. "You can trust me. Until we can figure this out, stay at my house."

Not sure how to respond to his offer and relieved that he no longer sounded angry, Lauren decided to ask, "Have you ever heard of Paul Johnson?"

"No, I don't think so. Who is he?"

Lauren wanted to see his reaction when she mentioned Paul. Watching his eyes, she felt pretty certain he was telling the truth.

"He worked with Omar, apparently for another company, and had some information about Omar. I was supposed to meet with him but he never showed up. That's the reason I came to Houston. To meet with Paul Johnson."

"Really?" Michael said in a questioning tone. "Could this Paul be something else and not what Jack told you? It's very suspicious that he never showed up to meet you."

"I thought so, too. I've been trying to text him but he hasn't responded."

"We'll check out his cell phone number also, when we need to."

"Do you really think Jack could be responsible for what happened to Omar and for planting explosives on the plane in Aspen?"

"It's possible. Maybe this Paul Johnson was Jack's partner and he is now blackmailing Jack, threatening to expose him. Jack's plan might have been to tell Paul he would meet with him, then fake his own death. He may have thought you knew he didn't get on the plane and you became a loose end. Maybe he sent you here to get you out of the way while he planned his escape. It's all speculation, but it's certainly something to think about. You have to realize that this is a shock for me, too."

Deep in thought, Lauren said, "I think I did see Jack after the plane left. I have always attributed it to my imagination, up until now. I guess it's possible that he knew I saw him." *What am I saying? I can't fall for this crazy speculation of Michael's.*

"I'm sorry, but you have to consider another point of view. You are blinded by your feelings for Jack. I can understand that. For a long time, I was blinded by the feelings I had for my wife. She and her lover lied to me for years. All humans are subject to denial. Everybody is vulnerable when it comes to being in relationships where they can get fooled. I'm no different. It's just human nature."

As Lauren studied Michael's somber expression, she realized that he had been deeply hurt by his failed marriage. He'd become cynical. She didn't know how to respond to his last comment. Part of her wanted to reach out to him and tell him that he could trust her. That she would never intentionally harm him. But she knew that she wasn't being completely honest with him now. When he found out the whole truth, he would probably never trust her again.

"I'll try to find out who Paul Johnson is," Michael said.

"I don't think he's a criminal," Lauren offered.

"You don't? Why is Paul Johnson alive and Omar dead? Maybe Johnson set him up. There were suspicions about soldiers and contractors distributing heroin. Perhaps Jack and Paul Johnson were in on some drug operation together. They could have been running a lucrative business on the side."

Lauren felt faint at the thought of what Michael was suggesting. Could this be true? Could everything she believed be completely opposite? She had to be open to the possibility that Jack was not telling her the truth. She'd been the only one who'd known he hadn't been on the plane that went missing. He'd even asked her not to tell her own sister.

She just wasn't cut out for this "cloak and dagger" stuff. Every way she looked at it, she was in trouble. She'd lied to the FBI and wondered how much trouble she was in for doing that alone. Worse, she might be harboring a criminal in her house.

The other scenario was just as bad. If Jack proved to be innocent and the victim of an attempted murder plot, whoever tried to kill him might try to kill her. That person could be Michael. Michael could be planning to kill her.

She stood up too quickly and thought she was going to faint. She was hungry and dehydrated and probably in a mild state of shock. Her hand went to her temple, and, as she started to sway, Michael rushed to her side and caught her, gently sitting her back down in the leather chair.

Realizing the degree of her distress, he disappeared, returning with a glass of water. Gently brushing the hair back from her face, he said calmly, "Don't worry, Lauren. You can trust me. I promise you, I didn't try to kill Jack, nor did I have anything to do with the bomb on the plane."

Lauren felt her composure returning and looked deep into his sincere brown eyes. She had to believe in someone, even if it ended up being a fatal mistake. Besides, how could she not trust Michael who seemed to care about her? She thought about how many men had put their lives in his hands when he was in the military. Now, with his business, young men counted on him to provide them with proper equipment and training. At this point she didn't feel she had a choice. He had taken her cell phone and he knew that Jack was alive.

"What should I do?" she asked.

"Let's check you out of your hotel room and I'll take you to my house. You'll be safe there."

Reluctantly, Lauren had agreed to go along with his plan, though she was frustrated at being in such a confused and vulnerable state. Michael was now calling the shots.

Michael took Lauren's cell phone from his desk and went down the hallway to find Joe. Not wanting to reveal details about Jack yet, he simply said, "Joe, can you have your friend who works at the phone company trace the last number called on this cell phone?

Specifically, I'd like to know the location of that cell phone." Joe looked at him with questioning eyes but didn't ask what was going on. Michael shot him a clear vibe not to ask.

Joe nodded. "Right away, sir."

Michael rejoined Lauren and they went to the reception area where Kate sat, clearly dumbfounded, wondering what was going on.

Addressing Kate, Michael said, "I know I don't have to tell you this, but please don't mention to anyone that the FBI was here."

Kate gave Michael an inquisitive look. She said, "Of course, sir, I understand."

"I knew that you would because this is especially important. I'll be back for my meeting later this afternoon. Lauren will not be returning today."

As they left the office and walked down the hall toward the elevator, Lauren said, "Kate is wondering what is going on. Maybe you should fill her in."

"I don't want to give anyone details about Jack or the FBI right now. It's not that I don't trust her. She's the best assistant I've ever had."

"She certainly made me feel welcome and comfortable. She's very professional and represents the company well." Lauren added thoughtfully, "It must be hard to work for a company of all men."

"I'm sure it is, especially when there's romance involved. She and Joe were an item for a while. They tried to keep it under wraps, but how can you think that you can seriously keep anything secret at a company that specializes in uncovering secrets?" Michael said with a slight smile. Lauren nodded. "I can see them as a couple," she said.

Lauren didn't say another word to Michael as they took the elevator to the underground parking lot and walked to his car. She continued her silence as they drove to the Hyatt. He held her hand to comfort her as they made their way through the hotel lobby toward the elevator. Inside the elevator he pushed the button to the sixth floor.

"Oh, I changed rooms. Remember? I'm on the third floor now," Lauren said as she pushed the button.

Michael glanced at her but didn't comment on the room change. Lauren used her key card to open the door and immediately began collecting her clothes and personal items. It didn't take her long to pack her bag and when she was finished they took the elevator to the lobby where Lauren checked out.

Someone watched from the corner of the lobby, hidden from view, as Lauren and Michael left the hotel. That someone had been waiting for Lauren to return.

CHAPTER 23

Once inside the BMW, traveling on the Interstate, Lauren's thoughts returned to the conversation she'd had with Elaine Jones. Elaine had seemed very interested in who the witness was that Lauren had come to Houston to meet. Since that time, Lauren reasoned that Elaine had known more than what she was telling her. She wondered how well Michael knew Elaine.

"Do you know Elaine Jones?" she asked suddenly.

The mention of Elaine's name clearly sparked an interest in Michael.

"Yes, I know that she's a reporter for the Houston Chronicle. She used to come by the office. Jack dated her for a short time, and that's why we hired her nephew, Ken, as our controller. He just resigned, which seems very suspicious now."

"He is her nephew?" *Of course, why didn't I figure that out? They have the same last name.*

"Yes, why?"

"Tuesday morning when I was eating breakfast. I read an article in the paper that Elaine wrote. I went to see her. I wanted to find out some information about your company and what happened to Omar. I don't think she was telling me everything she knew. If Ken is her nephew and he just resigned, maybe she does know something about what happened to Omar."

"Let's find out."

With that, Michael merged into the right lane so he could exit the Interstate. Veering back on to the freeway traveling in the opposite direction, he headed toward downtown.

Michael walked into the *Houston Chronicle* building like he owned the place—so self-assured—not like the cautious entrance Lauren had made two days ago. He walked right up to the receptionist and said in an authoritative voice, "Michael Dodson—here to see Elaine Jones. It's urgent."

The receptionist called Elaine without hesitation, and Elaine came down to greet them within a few minutes. She seemed surprised to see Lauren again and gave her a nod after greeting Michael.

"Let's go up to my office," she said, leading the way.

Inside Elaine's office, Michael and Lauren each took a seat while Elaine settled in behind her desk. She looked less confident than when Lauren had met with her. She shot Michael a nervous glance when he said, "Tell me everything you know about what's going on with Last Defense in Afghanistan and Omar's death. No more games."

It only took a few moments before she gave in. Elaine took a deep breath and began her story.

"Omar contacted me. He told me about drug use and trafficking in Afghanistan. He suspected that someone at Last Defense was involved, someone at the top. He didn't know who to turn to." Elaine hesitated.

"So he came to you." Michael said flippantly, "That worked out well for him."

Blood rushed to Elaine's face and her muscles visibly tightened as she said, "You cannot possibly blame what happened to Omar on me!"

"No, I'm sorry, of course not. How did you come to know Omar?"

"Jack and his dad were friends with Omar's family. Jack and I had dinner at the Kasim house a few times."

Michael nodded. "All right. Go on."

Elaine composed herself and then turned to Lauren with a broader explanation of the situation in Afghanistan.

"Afghanistan has been the greatest illicit opium producer in the entire world since the early nineties, except for one year when the Taliban ruled. Afghanistan supplies the world with heroin. In addition to opiates, it is also the largest producer of hashish in the world. You can't understand the country without knowing that poppy cultivation is the most prominent economic activity. Omar suspected that someone from Last Defense was in on the action."

"And you thought it was me," Michael said, as he looked at her with cold eyes.

"No, that's not true. Heroin traffickers have a symbiotic relationship with insurgents and terrorist groups such as the Taliban and al-Qaeda. Opium buys protection and pays for weapons and foot soldiers so that drug lords and insurgents can carry on their activities. Whoever is involved with this would be committing treason against the United States. I didn't think it could possibly be you—or anyone else from Last Defense, for that matter. I told Omar he had it wrong."

"What did Omar say to that?" Michael inquired.

"I think I convinced him that he was wrong about anyone at Last Defense being involved." Elaine looked out the window and then back to Michael. "So maybe I am partially responsible for what happened to him."

Lauren chimed in. "Why did Omar think that someone from Last Defense was involved?"

"He overheard some locals talking about a Mr. X. Rumors spread like wildfire, but Omar had a fairly good relationship with the locals. He was a Muslim and was someone they trusted, relatively speaking—if they trust anyone at all. They told him that Mr. X worked for a private contractor, not U.S. military personnel, although some of those were involved, too.

"You are not responsible for what happened to Omar," Michael said softly. "Remember that we still don't know what secrets Omar uncovered. Can you think of anything else that Omar said?"

"He told me he knew some Americans were drug smuggling because he'd seen soldiers and contractors moving around the province in American vehicles in the middle of the night. When he was in Herat province, the Northern alliance stronghold that borders Iran, he tried to find out if any of the vehicles were Last Defense issued.

"I wouldn't be surprised if drug smuggling was going on in that area. Heroin smuggling is prevalent there, along with heavy insurgent activity," Michael said casually, as if he were speaking of groceries being delivered.

"Omar said he turned in a full-length report about his suspicions to his supervisor, George Kaye. He also gave a copy of his report to a friend of his over there. I think his name was Johnson."

Lauren shot a glance over to Michael. He nodded to acknowledge that he recognized the name from their earlier conversation.

"Omar never received any feedback on his report," Elaine said.

"Was Omar concerned that there was never any action taken on his report of smuggling?" Lauren asked.

"A little but I guess he wasn't too surprised considering the corruption and bribery that goes on over there. Farmers routinely bribe police and other personnel to turn a blind eye. Law enforcement personnel are also paid off by drug traffickers to ignore or, in some cases, protect their movements. Even Afghan government officials are believed to be involved in opium trafficking."

"But he never told you that he suspected anyone in particular?" Lauren asked.

Elaine looked toward Lauren and spoke directly to her. "I'm sorry to tell you this, but he might have suspected Jack. That is probably why he contacted me. He knew of our intimate relationship and wanted me to reassure him that Jack would never be involved. He said that Jack was transferring him to a remote area. Also, Jack had been questioning his timesheets while he was stationed at Herat province, as if he was unaware that he was there. All this happened shortly after Omar turned in his report."

"That might have been a coincidence," Michael interjected. "A billing mix up occurred during that time. The agent from the Defense Department hadn't set up the appropriate purchase order paperwork for that operation, so the accountants didn't know why they were being billed for our contractors in that area. That was all cleared up and had nothing to do with smuggling. It was merely bureaucratic red tape."

"I guess Jack is in the clear, then. I am very happy to hear that—for the sake of his legacy," Elaine said, looking relieved.

"No, not so fast," Michael quickly added. "Jack then sent Omar to Faizabad, in Badakhsham province, which borders Tajikstan, Pakistan, and China. On his way there he was ambushed. So Jack is not in the clear, even though you both want him to be."

"That was the area that Jack was in charge of," Elaine interjected. "Maybe he wanted to send his best man there. Just because Jack transferred Omar there doesn't mean he planned the ambush."

"Does your nephew Ken know anything about this? Is that why he resigned?" Michael asked.

Elaine put her hand to her face and looked at Michael. "Ken . . . I wish . . ."

"Please tell us everything. It is important for us and for Ken."

"I told Ken everything I had heard from Omar. Ken said that he knew there were some suspicious billing irregularities at Last Defense. We compared notes, and he surmised that something was indeed going on. Then Ken had a bad idea . . ."

"Go on."

"Ken has a gambling problem and has debts to pay—debts he owes to bad people. I think his intention was blackmail.

His plan was to send Jack, Andy, Joe, you, other top level Last Defense personnel, and probably even Kate, anonymous letters, hoping to smoke out who was involved and get some payback money. Unfortunately, he's not any better at a blackmail attempt than at gambling. He sent each of you some cryptic message to let you know someone knew what was going on and was demanding money."

"Yes, I did receive something along that vein," Michael said. "I put it in my desk drawer for further review."

"Ken received a response—an envelope on his front door with a message in cut-out letters threatening his life. It shook him up badly because the note had come to his house, with his wife and baby home at the time. He has been in hiding with his family ever since. Then, when we heard that Jack was probably killed, we knew it couldn't be him."

Michael and Lauren exchanged glances.

CHAPTER 24

After learning everything they could from Elaine, Michael and Lauren left her office and again drove on the Interstate toward Michael's home, both too deep in thought to talk until Lauren began trying to put pieces of the puzzle together.

"Does Joe ever go out into the field? Has he ever been to Afghanistan?" Lauren asked.

"Joe has been to Afghanistan. He was also in the military and started work for us in the field but didn't like being called a mercenary. He'd gone to college to become a computer software programmer, so we pulled him from the field and put him in that position."

"Does he have an accounting degree as well?"

"He has taken accounting classes, so he's helping us look for a new controller. Joe is a brilliant and competent employee. Why, are you suspicious of him now?"

"I'm just thinking out loud. He seemed awfully suspicious of me earlier today, asking me questions about why I was here in Houston."

"I would trust Joe with my life. He was probably just reacting to a conversation that he had with our lawyers. He had a meeting with them late yesterday afternoon, and he probably mentioned you, which raised a red flag for them. They probably cautioned him against letting any outsiders into the office or giving them any information."

"Okay, that's probably it, then. Did you tell him anything when you gave him my cell phone? Did you tell him about Jack not being on the plane?"

"I'm not telling anyone about Jack right now. Let's try to keep things quiet for as long as we can."

"Trust no one," Lauren added.

"That's not it. It's just that rumors spread quickly, so it's always best to keep everyone on a need-to-know basis. That's a military term also."

"Understood."

"I do trust Joe. You're barking up the wrong tree if you think he would be involved in any of this. He grew up in a tough neighborhood in L.A. He learned at an early age how to defend himself and joined the military right out of high school."

"And you think that makes him above suspicion?"

"I guess no one is above suspicion, but his circumstances make him an unlikely candidate to get involved in drug smuggling. His brother got involved in the underworld, kind of like the Chinese mafia. He ended up getting killed by a rival gang at a fairly young age. I know that Joe was saddened and disgusted with his brother's life choices. His parents took the murder and their son's gang involvement very hard and now look to Joe to bring the family honor again. I can't see him following the same path as his brother. He knows where it leads."

"How about Andy?"

"I can't see Andy going rogue, either. He was a Navy SEAL and has devoted his life to his country. He had excellent letters of recommendation and has been a valued employee of Last Defense for a long time."

"It seems like you suspect Jack because he was never in the military, never in the club. Do you think that might be true?"

It looked like Lauren had just touched a nerve, but Michael calmly replied, "I have other reasons for suspecting Jack."

"So, please tell me. Why do you suspect Jack?" Then she added, her voice barely above a whisper, ". . . of selling out his country?"

Michael avoided her question. Had he tried evasion because he didn't want Lauren to know his innermost concerns?

Michael said, "It's hard to imagine Jack selling out his country or using our company to do it. Maybe Omar did have it wrong. Or a stray employee was on the take without any of the top personnel being aware of him. I'll check out George Kaye immediately. He was Omar's supervisor and now someone I suspect. As far as I was aware, he did his job well and was recently promoted."

"You can't keep track of all your employees at all times."

"We try to."

Lauren kept thinking about the innocent passengers on the plane. Maybe one of them hadn't been so innocent. Maybe one of them was a suicide bomber. Or, who was the target, if not Jack?

"Look," she said. "We are all making assumptions about the plane and we don't know if it has anything to do with us. Other people were on that plane, too. Important people. All this could just be a coincidence. Possibly someone else had an enemy. We've been so wrapped up in assuming the bomb on the plane was meant for Jack or that Jack placed it there to fake his own death that we're overlooking other possible scenarios."

"That's true. Perhaps the investigation will turn up a whole new suspect and intended victim. If so, we can all go back to our usual business and forget all about this."

Lauren suddenly thought about her job at the airport and what might be going on there.

"I need to contact my boss," she said. "I should have called in before now to check on things anyway. I can ask him what, if anything, he has found out. Maybe he knows something new about the investigation."

"You are quite an optimist."

"If that ends up being true, what's going to happen between you and Jack?" Lauren asked.

"To tell you the truth, I think Jack had been thinking about leaving Last Defense for a while now. What about Jack and you? Did seeing him stir up old feelings?" Michael took his eyes off the road and looked directly at Lauren. "Do you think you'll still want me to come to Aspen?"

She briefly looked at him in with surprise. *He really is interested in me romantically.*

"I don't know," Lauren said. She turned away and pretended to watch the traffic beyond the side window.

CHAPTER 25

Lauren considered telling Michael about the letter from Ali Kasim but decided against it. Some level of propriety had to be maintained. The letter was addressed to Jack. Ali wanted to talk to Jack. It would seem like a violation to show it to Michael.

It wasn't long before they entered a residential neighborhood and parked in the driveway of Michael's house, which Lauren immediately decided was beautiful. It was located in a new housing development in Humble, a classy Houston suburb. The brick ranch home wasn't ostentatious, but new and spacious. A small yard was covered with a carpet of meticulously cared-for grass. He'd had the interior professionally decorated, and Lauren immediately felt comfortable and at home in it.

"This is a beautiful house. You have excellent taste," Lauren said as she admired the artwork on the walls and a Lalique vase on the coffee table.

"What were you expecting? *Dogs Playing Poker?*" which made her laugh. "Come with me and I'll show you the spare bedroom where you can put your things."

Lauren followed him toward a cozy guest bedroom with its own ien-suite bathroom.

After helping Lauren with her bag, both took a seat on the bed. Michael insisted that she cancel her plans to fly back to Aspen in the afternoon.

"I'm concerned about your safety, Lauren," he told her. "It's imperative you stay in a protected place."

Lauren felt that she had no choice but to agree. He handed her his cell phone so that she could call the airline and cancel her flight. He then took back his phone and dropped it in his pocket.

"When will I get my cell phone back?" Lauren asked.

"Joe is tracing Jack's location. We'll find out where he is. I'll bring it when I come back later tonight. You do want to find out where he is, don't you?"

"Yes," Lauren said as she fingered the lovely blue comforter they were sitting on. She looked down, and then at him.

Lauren saw that Michael could sense her apprehension. Sure enough, to reassure her about his intentions, he said, "Lauren, now that I know about you and Jack, I won't try anything. I assume, with Jack, you must be feeling confused and vulnerable. I would never try to take advantage of the situation. And look—there's a lock on the bedroom door." He smiled as he pointed to the doorknob on the interior door, which did feature a sturdy lock.

"Thanks, I appreciate that." she said. *Yeah, like a lock on the door would keep you out. It hasn't in the past.*

"I'm glad you noticed I'm a gentleman," he said in a causal tone.

Lauren realized that Michael was trying to make her comfortable, but she also knew that Michael always planned very carefully. She wasn't stupid. She was worried because the best way to bring Jack out of hiding was to remove Jack's ability to contact her.

"There is something else I want to tell you," Michael said in a serious tone.

"Sure. What is it?"

"You know the software program we use to measure the

honesty and integrity of potential employees?"

"Yes. I took the test, I remember."

"We used it on ourselves a few months ago."

Lauren nodded. "And?"

"Jack failed."

Michael glanced at his watch. "I'm sorry to leave you like this, but I have to go back to the office to meet with a client. It's a more casual client and one you would approve of. Then I need to browse through some personnel files. After that, I'll check in with Joe to see if he has found out where Jack is. Once we locate him, we'll get some answers."

"Who's the client? Or is it top secret?"

He playfully tapped his finger on her nose. "You watch too many movies. I won't be long. Remember, I told you that we're expanding our business. Get yourself something to eat. You'll feel better. There's food and beer in the refrigerator and frozen meals in the freezer. Regular bachelor fare, but I think you'll find something that you'll like. I'll be home by dinner time with your cell phone, and then, if you'd like, we'll go out to eat."

"Before you leave, can you tell me where your phone is so I can call my boss?"

"I don't have a landline. Here, go ahead and use my cell. I'd like to hear what he has to say also."

He watched her punch in the number to David Richards' direct line.

"Hi, David. It's Lauren. How's it going there? How are you holding up?"

"We've got everything under control here. Everyone is doing a great job. How are you doing?"

Lauren didn't know if he was telling the truth or not. Her boss would lie to keep her from feeling bad, no matter how hectic things were. He would say he was fine if the airport was on fire, just to spare her feelings.

"Houston is a nice city. I can't complain. David, I called to

159

ask you if you've gotten any updates about the plane. I found out that it was a small explosive device that brought it down. Have you heard anything about that?"

"That's the same story we've been told. There are no survivors. I'm sorry, Lauren. The only thing that's been released to the press is that the plane has been found. How did you find out about the bomb?"

Lauren was stuck for an answer. "Long story. I heard through Jack Kelly's business associates. They must have an inside connection to the investigation. What else have you heard?"

"A Denver local news anchor and her husband, a Saudi national who was a former ambassador to the United States, were onboard the plane, as you know. The authorities are looking into him and a possible motive there. He was probably the intended victim. They're still investigating, but that's what I think."

"Really?" Lauren couldn't hide her relief that there was a real possibility Jack was not the intended victim or the perpetrator, although she felt deeply sorry for the victims of the plane crash and their families.

"How is Jack Kelly's family doing?"

David hasn't been told yet that Jack wasn't on the plane. They must have a reason for keeping that information secret. What will he think when he finds out? Will he be angry? I guess I'll cross that bridge when I come to it.

"His family's okay. Thanks again for letting me leave work to come here. I'll be back there on Saturday to help with the normal travel rush and the fallout from the plane crash. I'm leaving Houston today." She looked over at Michael. "I mean tomorrow. Anyway, I'll be there on Saturday, come hell or high water. I miss home."

"Okay, I'll see you Saturday. We miss you, too, see you soon."

In truth, David Richards felt overwhelmed and had been working long hours to keep up with his job and the investigation. If the Saudi national was the intended victim of the plane crash, the public relations nightmare would never end. The spotlight shining on Aspen and the airport would prove disastrous to everyone who worked there. Wanting more time with his family, he'd promised them before the plane went missing on Saturday that they would spend Sunday and Monday together skiing and watching movies, sharing quality time together as a family.

His teenage son and daughter needed more time with their dad. They weren't bad kids, but they weren't valedictorians, either. Neither of them seemed to be athletically inclined, which seemed odd since both of their parents were expert skiers. He could feel his family slipping away from him as he worked long hours with little time off to be with them.

And it didn't look like things were going to change anytime soon. The investigators wanted to interview all the airport employees. The interviews and ongoing investigation would take days, weeks, or even months to complete. Just one more thing to be going on at this stressed-out busy airport, running at full capacity just to keep up with the travel demands of the resort.

He looked at the phone he had just hung up. Thank God Lauren would be back on Saturday. Glancing at his watch, he realized it was time to get ready for his interview with the NTSB.

CHAPTER 26

Aspen, Colorado

The investigators from the NTSB asked David Richards to set up an interview room where they could question all the employees at the airport. After he'd set up the area, David was their first interviewee. He sat down at a table across from two agents, too tired to be nervous. Only one agent asked the questions while the other took notes.

"Mr. Richards, we will need you to provide a timeline of your day on Saturday. You will need to account for every single hour here. Also, please provide us a list of all your airport employees, and indicate the ones who were working that day. We'll need a timeline of all their activities as well."

"Yes, I understand. I'll get everything ready. But you are aware that the plane was a private corporate charter, so the passengers didn't go through the normal TSA security procedures, right? Most of our employees would have had little or no contact with . . ."

The investigator cut him off. "Do you know if any of your employees have ever worked for Hewlett Packard in the past? One of the passengers was a top level executive with Hewlett Packard.

"No, I don't know that offhand. Our Human Resources department can research that."

"We will need a list of all previous employers of all your employees, too."

Is that all? That will only take hundreds of man hours, David wanted to shout out what he was thinking but kept quiet.

"Are there any employees that haven't showed up for work since Saturday?"

"Just one. One of my assistants, Lauren Reese, went to Houston because she had a close connection with someone on the plane and wanted to be with his family. She left on Monday."

"What passenger was on the plane that she knew?"

"Jack Kelly. He was a family friend, originally from Colorado. They went to school together."

The two agents exchanged quick glances but said nothing.

"She'll be back on Saturday. I also have her cell phone number if you need that."

"Give us her phone number after we're done here. On Saturday we'll need to formally interview her as soon as she lands. We'll also need her home address."

David was perplexed about why the focus on Lauren, but once again, he said nothing.

"Okay, I'll get her address for you. Everyone else has shown up to work as usual. All employees here have had intensive background checks. I'm sure you won't find any irregularities."

"Do you know anything about Mr. Shah, the Saudi national that was onboard the plane?"

"No."

"He has written a number of articles, some of them controversial. He writes about Muslims in America and the problems they face. Do you have any reason to believe that would upset anyone here?"

"No. Not at all."

"Could you make up an interview schedule for all your employees? We don't want to disrupt operations here more than necessary, but I'm sure you understand that we need to thoroughly investigate this case."

"Absolutely. I'll have HR get right on it."

"Do you know if any of your employees have financial problems or are involved with drugs?"

"No. This is an expensive place to live, but everyone seems to make ends meet. As far as drugs go, no, we require mandatory drug screening for pre-employment, and I haven't noticed any problems that would be related to drug use."

"Are there any employees here that are not U.S. citizens and working on a green card?"

"I don't think so, but I can have Human Resources check that out, too."

One of the agents brought out a few files from his briefcase. Looking up through his reading glasses, he pulled out the top one and asked David, "Are you a U.S. citizen?"

"I have just become one. I'm originally from Canada."

The agent perusing the file made David more uncomfortable. He had no idea where the file had come from or why the agent had it in his possession.

"I married a U.S. citizen, and so have become one myself," David added.

The agent closed the file.

"Some of your employees look foreign."

"We don't ask about religion or national origin—by law—if that's what you're getting at."

"We just want your opinion and cooperation. Did you know what type of business Jack Kelly was in?"

"Not really. I know he was with Last Defense. What exactly did he do?"

The agents explained all about Jack Kelly's activities and then asked if anyone there might have a problem with him or his business. David answered in the negative, and after about another half hour of questioning, they told him he was free to go back to work.

"I hope you realize this is just a formality. We need to find out if anyone working here would have a motive to sabotage the plane," the agent said in closing.

"Yes, I understand. I want to help in any way I can. The sooner the resolution, the sooner we can return to normal operations." *And I can take a day off.*

Chapter 27

It wasn't long before David Richards was called back into the interview room. He obligingly sat down again for another interview session, coffee in hand.

"Mr. Richards, we have been informed that you had lunch on Friday with the Denver news anchor woman that was onboard the plane. You didn't mention that you knew her in our last interview."

"You didn't ask me if I knew her. You asked if I knew her husband, which I didn't."

"How did you know her?"

"I used to be on the Canadian Olympic ski team. That was years ago, and at the time, Jenn did a story on me. We got to know each other and have been friends through the years. This is her favorite place to ski."

"Why didn't you invite your spouses to the lunch?"

"No particular reason. It was impromptu. She came to my office and asked if I wanted to have lunch. Catch up."

"Were you having an affair with her?"

"No."

"What did you talk about?"

"Just old times and what had been going on in our lives. She had only been married for a few years and was having marital issues due to the cultural differences she and her husband came to the marriage with . . . but I think they were working things out."

"Did your wife know that you had lunch with Jennifer Summers?"

"No."

"Why not?"

"I don't tell her about everyone I have lunch with. There was no reason to tell her."

"Did you harbor any bad feelings toward Ms. Summers?"

"No. I loved . . . I was very fond of her."

"Do you think Mr. Shah was aware of your lunch, or your relationship?"

"I don't think so, no."

"What do you think he would have done if he found out?"

"Nothing. I'm sure he has female friends. I don't think he would have put a bomb on the plane to kill them both, if that's what you're suggesting."

The investigators stared at David.

"Okay, that's all, the investigator said. Please keep us informed of anything you can think of that would be relevant to the case."

"I will, thanks."

With that affirmation, David got up and left the room.

CHAPTER 28

Back in Houston, Lauren told Michael what she'd found out about the news anchor and the woman's husband.

"That should keep the investigators busy for a long time. At least, it takes suspicion and attention away from us, so that's good," Michael said.

Michael took back his cell phone. "Okay. I've got to go to my meeting, but I'll be back soon."

Watching Michael leave, Lauren felt like a prisoner in a beautiful house. She decided her confusion wasn't going to clear up any time soon. She still wasn't sure whom to trust, but it seemed best to play along with Michael. She had to admit that he'd gotten her to trust him, but whether he was a good liar or an honest man remained to be seen. She felt lost without her cell phone.

She couldn't call Jack, or anyone else, for that matter. What would Michael do when he found out Jack was in Aspen? Would he still believe that she didn't know where Jack was, and would he ever trust her again?

Lauren wasn't hungry, but she had to eat something to keep up her strength. She heated up a frozen entrée in the microwave. Looking around the kitchen, she decided it was too manly, it needed a woman's touch. Michael must have just recently bought the house, after his divorce.

Then she wondered if she would ever share a home with a real, reliable and honest man. *Do any men exist that don't have secrets?* Now she was spending the night in a house with another man. It had been difficult enough with Jack a few nights ago, and now the thought of Michael in the next room both excited and scared her. She decided she had gone way too long without a man's touch and remembered that Andy had warned her not to get involved with Michael, given his newly divorced state of mind.

Her last boyfriend had been such a disappointment. That was one of the reasons she'd moved to Aspen when the opportunity presented itself. Kismet, she thought, and a chance to get away from Denver and the memory of Dale, a relationship that had hurt her deeply. *Another guy that put my heart in a blender and pushed the frappe button. Will I ever find the right man? Is this the right place to look?*

After eating the light lunch, desperate for entertainment and contact with the everyday world, Lauren turned on the flat screen television in Michael's living room. While channel surfing, she found a small claims court show that had a plaintiff and defendant battling over some minor dispute. She thought it seemed petty compared to her current situation, so she changed the station. A soap opera was next. Maybe she could relate to that. She watched about ten minutes of the show.

Lauren turned her thoughts to Shannon who would be wondering where her sister was and why she hadn't called. If only she could call Shannon to let her know she was safe and just delayed another day in Houston? But was she really safe? At least she'd confided in Shannon. But why get Shannon more involved now? Why tell her anything else about Last Defense when information only seemed to get people killed? She would rather have an angry sister than a dead sister. She felt like she was in Omar's position, not knowing whom to trust. Would she and Omar share the same fate?

She sincerely hoped that Michael didn't intend to do her harm.

But wouldn't he have done her in by now if that was his intention? Or maybe he was keeping her as a hostage to get Jack back. What if he called Jack using her cell phone and then told him he could have her back for a large ransom?

Another scenario—what if Jack and Michael were in this together and they were both conspiring, trying to figure out what to do with her since she'd learned too much about Last Defense?

To get her mind off her dismal thoughts, she opened her purse to check how much cash she had. She would need some for her trip home. As she fished for her wallet, it hit her. The letter addressed to Jack from Ali Kasim was gone! *I'm sure I put it back in my purse after I read it to Jack.* She rummaged frantically through every compartment, but realized it was gone. *Oh my God, what's next?*

CHAPTER 29

The ringing of the doorbell made Lauren jump. *Who could it be?* Possibilities ran through her mind as she crept over to answer the door. She looked through the security peephole and gasped in astonishment. Jack Kelly stood on the other side.

Taking a deep breath to calm herself down, she opened the door.

"Jack! What are you doing here? How did you find me? I thought you were still in Aspen."

"I expected a better welcome. You don't seem happy to see me. Has Michael gotten to you? What has he told you?"

"I'm just surprised, that's all. When did you leave Aspen?"

"I left bright and early yesterday morning. I didn't get much sleep Tuesday night after I talked to you." He added sarcastically, "After your date."

Lauren let that one pass.

"I just got in today. I was on the road when you called to tell me about Ali's letter yesterday, and I was here when you called earlier to tell me about the FBI. Did you really think I could stay in Aspen knowing you were in imminent danger in Houston?"

"How did you get out of Aspen? Certainly you didn't fly."

"I drove here—in your jeep. I had enough cash on hand to

pay for gas and a hotel so I could get a few hours' sleep last night."

"What have you been doing since you got here?"

"Okay, I lied when I told you that I hadn't heard from Paul Johnson. I sent him a cryptic text that said "still alive" from my new phone Tuesday evening. He was smart enough to realize my cell phone had been hacked and someone knew I was planning to meet with him. He sent me a text late Tuesday night after I talked to you. I told him not to contact you or return your messages because I wanted you to leave Houston and remove yourself from danger. You were already in deeper than I ever imagined you could be."

"So that's why Paul didn't answer any of my text messages. Didn't you think I would wonder? I can't believe you would tell Paul not to contact me," Lauren said, exasperated. "Why would you mislead me like that?"

"I thought you would be back in Colorado by now. If you'd followed my instructions, you would have known about Paul," Jack said heatedly. In a calmer voice, he asked, "At least, may I come inside and maybe sit down and tell you everything?"

Reluctantly, Lauren opened the door wide and stepped aside to let him in.

She led Jack into the living room and they both sat down on the couch.

"After you called about the FBI today," Jack continued to explain, "I had Paul call the Last Defense office to ask for you, saying he was your brother-in-law. Kate said that you and Michael had left. I thought that Michael would drop you off at your hotel room and you would check out. I waited for you in the lobby, but then saw you were with him. I didn't want a confrontation in the lobby of the hotel with Michael. At least not until I have more evidence against him. After you both left, I couldn't get in your jeep fast enough to follow you. I just assumed he would take you to the airport. But you never showed up. Then I took a chance and came here. Where is Michael, by the way?"

"He went back to the office for a meeting with a client."

"Why didn't you call me as soon as he left?"

"I would have called you right away but Michael took my cell phone. Michael knows you're still alive. He was with me when the FBI told us you weren't on the plane. He figured out that I called you and he took my cell phone so that he could have Joe's friend track where you were. He used my cell phone to locate your cell phone . . . and you."

Jack immediately took his cell phone from his jacket pocket, and pulled out the battery.

"Now he won't find me."

Lauren smiled. Jack once again had the upper hand in this crazy cat-and-mouse game.

"Why did he bring you here instead of taking you to the airport?"

"He said it was to protect me . . . from you," Lauren said as she looked in his eyes.

"That sounds like him. What a control freak. We can't stay here. He may be coming back soon. Get your things. I'll tell you more in the car."

Lauren didn't want Jack to realize that she now had doubts about him. Michael had raised some plausible theories. She would go with Jack, but she would be careful, still not sure she could trust him.

She led Jack to the spare bedroom so that he could grab her suitcase. They left the house and got into Lauren's jeep. "How do you like my car?" Lauren asked Jack as he opened the passenger door for her.

"I like it. It reminds me of Colorado, and it reminds me of you."

Jack drove out of the cul-de-sac and onto the main street.

"Where are we going, Jack? It's too late for me to catch a flight to Denver and then connect on to Aspen."

"I don't know, I'll come up with something. I don't think it would be safe to go to my condo. I'm staying at a hotel but it may not be the best place for you. And it only has one bed."

Lauren gave him a "cool it" look.

"Still mad about Johnson, huh?"

"Why don't you take me back to the Hyatt? I felt safe there. Some of the staff even know me by name now."

"Do you really think that would be a good idea? That would be the first place Michael or anyone else would look for you. And the hotel clerk would probably tell Michael what room you were in. How about the Marriott next to the airport?"

"Okay, that sounds good. I can take a shuttle in the morning, fly to Denver and then go back home to Aspen."

"Tell me more about Paul Johnson," Lauren said as they got closer to the Marriott. "Who is he? Why didn't he meet me? I thought I saw him come into the bar and walk toward me, but then he turned around and walked away." *Who is he really and how do you know him?*

"Paul saw Michael in the hotel lobby when he came to meet you. He had met him once in Afghanistan. The more he thought about it as he approached the bar, the more it seemed like a trap. He didn't know why Michael would be at the hotel or who else might be waiting for him."

"So he thinks Michael is involved in what's going on?"

"Yes, we both do. What do you think?"

Lauren shook her head. "I don't think Michael would be involved."

Jack shot here a quick glance. "I'm sure Michael has romanced and charmed you. He's probably even done more than that. You haven't...have you?"

"No. He's been a perfect gentleman." *Not that he hasn't tried.*

Lauren noticed that Jack couldn't hide the fact that he felt relieved. It showed on his face, and she inwardly smiled.

"We must not be talking about the same guy. I could hear in your voice Tuesday night that you were a little smitten."

"Stop."

"Well, besides wanting to get into your pants, I would bet my bottom dollar that he also wanted to find out if I had told you anything . . . about the company, about him, and about Omar."

"I guess that's probably true."

"By the way, do you have that letter from Omar's dad? I want to show it to Paul. I told him about it."

"Actually, no. I looked in my purse shortly before you showed up and it wasn't there."

Again, Jack took his eyes off the road for a moment to look at Lauren. He said, "Michael must have taken it from your purse. Now do you think he's as innocent as you believe?"

"Perhaps not."

"Did you tell him about the letter?"

"No, the letter was addressed to you, for your eyes only. I didn't feel I had the right to share it with anyone but you. Don't you trust my integrity?"

"Of course I do and I have some other news that you might be interested in. Michael was in Afghanistan when Omar was killed. He often traveled to Afghanistan with no explanation as to why, not even to me. I asked but I could never get an answer from him."

"Was he actually in the area where Omar was ambushed?"

Jack rolled his eyes and didn't answer her question.

"Do you really think Michael was the sniper? That he would kill one of his own men?"

No answer. They pulled into the check-in area of the Marriott, which featured an awning and a pedestrian walkway, then exited the jeep and walked into the lobby. Lauren told the clerk at the front desk that she'd like to rent a room for the night and book a seat on the shuttle for the morning ride to the airport. He was happy to accommodate her request

The fourth-floor room was small, but this was her last night in Houston so it would do just fine. It afforded one closet, a bathroom, a king size bed, end tables with lamps and two plush chairs with a large ottoman between them. A desk and functional chair sat by the sliding glass door which opened onto a small balcony. Lauren sat on the bed while Jack sat down in one of the chairs.

"Please tell me more about Paul Johnson. Who is he?" Lauren asked. She figured if she asked enough times, maybe she'd get the real answer.

"He was a paid informant working with the CIA."

"What? I thought you told me earlier that he was another contractor."

"I was wrong. I didn't know myself at the time that he was working with the CIA. Why? What are you suggesting?"

"Nothing. Go on."

"Paul was in Afghanistan to investigate insurgent activity. He ran into Omar, whom he had gone to school with at West Point. Omar confided in him suspicions about a drug trafficking ring involving some soldiers and contractors in Afghanistan. Omar and Paul were together when they overheard some Army soldiers talking about drugs and how to transfer them out of the county. Omar wrote a report about what he had seen and heard and turned a copy over to Paul, saying he had given the original report to his supervisor at Last Defense. Paul didn't think too much about it until Omar was killed. At that time, Paul became suspicious that the leader of the ring was someone Omar knew and that Omar was killed because he was getting close to the truth. There's only one person the leader could be, and that would have to be Michael. He's the only one who holds that much power and influence. He has travelled there many times with no explanation of why, not even to me. I asked but I could never get an answer from him. With his resume, he would be trusted and his character beyond reproach. That would give him the opportunity."

"So, the report is what Paul wanted to give you, right?"

"Yes, he wanted to hand it over to me personally."

"So, it is just speculation that the leader of this drug smuggling ring is Michael. Neither of you are sure, right? Omar never mentioned any names."

Jack shrugged. "No, Omar did not mention a name. Why are you so reluctant to believe that Michael might be involved? What spell does he have over you?"

"He seemed sincere, that's all," Laruen said, not willing to admit how much time she had spent with Michael and how intimate they had become.

"Right, well, facts are facts. Anyway, back to Paul. He was pulled off his assignment in Afghanistan and transferred back home. He felt that the only way he could ever sleep again was if he tried to obtain justice for Omar, thus our agreed upon meeting."

"Has he given you the report?"

"Yes, today, but I haven't had a chance to go through it yet. If you were home in Colorado, I could be reading it right now."

"Okay, okay. Why did Paul contact you?"

"Ali told Paul that I could be trusted and that I would investigate the matter, as a family friend."

"What are you going to do now? Did you ever contact the FBI?"

"Give me Agent Stafford's number and I'll call him today. I have something to tell you. I've decided to go to Afghanistan myself. I have a lot of arrangements to make before I leave tomorrow morning. It's risky, but that's the only way I can be certain of what happened there. This has to be resolved, and it will be. Paul has given me names of operatives still there who will help me."

Lauren took out Agent Stafford's card from her purse and wrote down the number on a piece of hotel stationary. As she gave it to Jack, she asked, "Why didn't Paul ever say anything to his superiors or the CIA about Omar's report?"

"Investigating drug smuggling wasn't Paul's assignment. Like I said, he didn't think much about it until Omar was killed. He was lucky to get out of Afghanistan."

"Yes, I guess you could say he was lucky." Lauren remembered Michael's comment about Omar being killed, but Paul Johnson making it out of Afghanistan alive. Jack didn't notice if Lauren was suggesting anything other than being lucky.

"Paul contacted me often at Last Defense, and we weren't as careful as we should have been about keeping our communication under wraps," Jack said. He never mentioned that he was with the CIA, but he did tell me that he wanted to turn over a report to me. I think everyone at Last Defense realized that I was investigating the case and that I had an informant. Our lawyers had told us not to talk with anyone about the case, especially a potential witness for the Kasim family. I was working against my own company, my own interest, but I had to. I think anyone would have, under the circumstances."

"I was talking to Joe earlier, and he said that Ken Jones quit. Joe mentioned that you were working with him about some billing issue," Lauren said, trying to probe Jack for more information from his side of the story.

"Ken quit? He was our controller. He probably quit because he didn't feel safe after the plane went missing. He may have had suspicions about improprieties and knew something wasn't legit. Maybe someone asked him to do something he didn't think was ethical. He's the nephew of a reporter here in Houston, Elaine Jones. Maybe Elaine knows something. I might try to contact her."

Lauren noticed that Jack never mentioned he had received any blackmail notes. He also didn't address his previous intimate relationship with Elaine Jones. Was he being evasive? He still didn't seem to be telling her everything, which didn't make her less suspicious of him. Jack stood up to leave, and Lauren walked with him to the door.

"I'm sorry I have to leave," he said. "Believe me, I wouldn't go if I wasn't sure that you are safe here. No one knows where you are, even so, don't answer the phone. Don't open the door. Be safe, take the shuttle to the airport in the morning. And for God's sake, get on the plane!"

"Okay, Jack. I'll follow your instructions. Thanks for bringing me here. I feel so much better now. I understand things more clearly." Lauren said, relief showing in her face. *I almost made a terrible mistake.*

"That's good. I should have told you more over the phone days ago. I'm sorry."

"I'm worried about you. Please be careful. Remember, I came here to help you and now you have rescued me. Do you really have to go to Afghanistan?"

"Yes. Since I don't know whom I can trust, I have to go. Ironically, I'll feel safer there than here since I'll have CIA cover."

"That's what Omar told his dad, that he didn't know whom he could trust."

Jack smiled and look relieved. He went to hug her, but she instinctively pulled away.

"First you thought I was a womanizer and a cad. Now someone has you thinking I'm a drug smuggler and a murderer. I can't seem to win with you. Lauren, I don't know what Michael has told you about me but if what he told you about me was true, would I be here now?"

"You're right. You wouldn't be here if what Michael said about you was true."

"When will you listen to your own heart instead of other people? I will win you back, Lauren. This mess will be over soon. I'm not going to let you get away again."

Lauren opened the door and watched as he walked down the hall. She went back inside her room, locked the deadbolt and the security latch. *I'm safe. No one knows I'm here . . . except Jack, and he will probably tell Paul Johnson.*

Michael was surprised when he returned to his house around four o'clock and found Lauren gone. He noticed her bag was missing as well. What were the circumstances surrounding her departure? Had she found a way to contact Jack? Searching his house thoroughly, he didn't see any signs of a struggle. If his hopes and suspicions were right, Lauren had probably managed to get a taxi, eliciting the help of a neighbor, and was now at the airport waiting for a flight back to Colorado. He had her cell phone in his hand and was anxious to tell her that Jack was in Houston. Or did she already know?

She obviously wasn't going to reveal everything she knew and he wasn't about to try any hardcore interrogation methods on her. She was a woman that he could easily develop affection for, if circumstances were different. He was convinced that she'd stepped out of her comfortable life to help Jack. How many women would do that?

Deep in thought, Michael drew his cell phone and FBI Agent Stafford's card from his breast pocket. But as he began to punch in Stafford's number, he suddenly aborted the call, tossing the card and the phone on the table. After pouring himself a stiff scotch and water, he sat down to think things through one more time. Considering all the facts, he came to a conclusion and decided to call his office.

"Kate, please arrange a flight to Afghanistan first thing tomorrow. Also, get hold of Colonel Shore and tell him to be expecting me."

CHAPTER 30

After a restless night's sleep, the ringing phone on the desk startled Lauren awake the next morning. She looked at the clock on the nightstand and gasped when she saw it read eight o'clock. She still must be on Colorado time. Even though Jack had warned her not to answer the phone, she got up and, walking over to the desk, picked up the receiver.

"I thought I told you not to answer the phone," Jack said on the other end of the line.

"I know, but you're the only one that knows I'm here. Besides, it could have been the front desk telling me something important. The place could be on fire, for all I know. No one is going to hurt me over the phone."

"I'm glad you did answer. I wanted to tell you something."

"What?"

"Ali Kasim was killed last night."

"Oh, my God, that's terrible. What happened?" Feeling weak in the knees, Lauren sat down in the chair at the desk.

"He was shot at close range by a sniper. He never had a chance. He died before the ambulance arrived. His wife said that someone had called, and afterward Ali seemed anxious and upset. He left the house in a rush without telling her where he was going or who he was meeting. He seemed upset and shaken. He was shot when he got out of his car at the strip mall in front of a coffee house. I'm suspicious. I called Paul, and we agree that it was not a random shooting. We think it was an assassination. Paul was especially concerned after hearing about the letter Ali sent to me. The police are investigating."

"I can't believe it—someone killed him."

"I wish I could have come by to tell you the news personally but I'm getting ready to leave. Lauren, you know, I have to go. It's the only way. I'm scheduled to attend a criminal investigative meeting at an Army compound in Afghanistan. I wanted to call anyway, to say goodbye, until we meet again."

Lauren was worried, but understood what Jack was telling her. He had taken special care to make sure she was safe and now he had to do what he felt was necessary. She wanted to ask when she would see him again but decided against it.

"Paul is taking me to the airport, and a CIA plane will transport me to Afghanistan. At least I have their support now. The FBI has been informed as to what's going on, so don't worry about them. Agent Stafford didn't think you were telling the truth when he met you in Michael's office, by the way. You aren't a good liar, and it was very transparent that you were hiding something. Now he understands why. He'll give you a ride to the airport. Why don't you give him a call?"

"I don't need an escort. I think I can manage getting to the airport and on a plane by myself. I'll take the hotel shuttle."

"Lauren, you have a bad habit of not doing what I tell you to do. I truly have your best interest in mind. You always seem to find trouble. That includes, but is not limited to, getting involved with me," Jack was teasing, but also dead serious, she knew. "I want Agent Stafford to be your escort to Colorado, to Aspen, to your house, and then tuck you in bed if necessary. Tell you what. I'll call him myself and tell him to pick you up as soon as he has a chance."

"Okay, Jack, thanks. It seems like I just said this to you, but

I'll say it again, please be careful."

He promised that he would, and with that, they said their goodbyes and she hung up the phone, amazed at the things she had gone through over the past few days. Finding Jack, then thinking she'd lost him, and now she could lose him again. She wanted, no she deserved, a second chance to get to know Jack.

Her thoughts went back to Ali Kasim. How could she find out more about the events of last night? She took out a business card from her purse, but it wasn't Agent's Stafford's she grabbed, it was Elaine Jones'.

Elaine answered her phone right away. She had listed several numbers on her card and Lauren figured that her cell number would be the best one to call to get an immediate response.

"Hi, Elaine. This is Lauren Reese, Jack's friend from Colorado."

"Yes, of course I know who you are." Elaine sounded like she was growing tired of Lauren's innocent act, so Lauren dropped it and became more direct.

"When I first met you the other day, why didn't you tell me that your nephew worked at Last Defense?"

"I didn't know you. I didn't even know if you were who you said you were. I called Ken right away after you left to tell him about you. He had never heard of you, which he should have if you were who you said you were. So I became suspicious. Now you know why. Now you know the whole story."

"I just found out that Ali Kasim, Omar's father, was shot and killed last night. I would like to know if you have heard anything about it?"

"I did hear about the shooting. I called my contact at the police department right away when I heard it on the news this morning."

"What did he say?"

"Why should I give you any information?"

"Maybe we can compare notes. We aren't enemies. We need to work together."

"Okay, point taken. I'll tell you. My sources are telling me that Ali's murder looks like it was a hit, not a random shooting or a robbery. This is confidential information. We're not releasing anything official at this time, so please don't tell anyone. Not even Michael. Is Michael there with you?"

"You've just told me what I feared. No, Michael isn't here. I haven't seen him since yesterday afternoon. Speaking of Michael, do you still believe that he couldn't be involved in any of this?"

"I don't really know. Whoever it is, they're three steps ahead of everyone else. How do you know about Ali?"

"I found a letter in Jack's mailbox. It was from Ali. I opened it and read it. He said in the letter that he knew who was responsible for the death of his son."

Elaine gasped. "Why didn't you contact Ali right away?"

"I tried to, but he was out of town. That's why I stayed in Houston, for a chance to meet with him. But then, I got sidetracked."

"Yes, I think I know who sidetracked you. Where are you now?"

"I'm staying at the Marriott by the airport. I'm getting ready to leave for Colorado today."

"That's a good idea, Lauren. You need to be safe, too. All of your concern about others, and you are in the thick of it yourself. Come to think of it, so am I. Maybe I should go with you," Elaine said, jokingly, but serious.

"Thanks, Elaine. You're right. You better watch your back, too. Thanks for the information. If I find out anything more, I'll let you know, and if you do, please call me." But then she remembered she still didn't have her cell phone. She didn't want to explain to Elaine why Michael had taken it from her, because then she'd have to reveal that Jack was alive and well in Houston. *Or does Elaine already know? She still seems to be hiding something.* She gave Elaine her home phone number in Aspen, telling her she would be there later in the evening.

After Lauren hung up the phone, she felt sad for Ali and his family. They had now lost a son and a father. Then a shadow of grief and guilt overwhelmed her. Did finding the letter that Ali sent to Jack contribute to his murder? She had strong regrets about opening the letter. She had been careless, and now Ali had been gunned down.

A quick shower couldn't wash away her feelings of guilt. Slipping into her jeans and blouse, she sat down at the desk. She listed on the hotel stationary pad the people who knew about the letter. The letter was the key. The report that Paul had was inconclusive. Omar didn't suspect anyone in particular. Ali had figured out who murdered his son because he had a piece of the puzzle that no one else had. If her carelessness in handling the letter had caused Ali Kasim to be shot by a sniper, the least she could do was help bring the shooter to justice. She hoped writing things down would help her understand.

She wrote:

Paul . . . *Jack told him about the letter. Maybe he isn't who Jack thinks he is.*

Michael . . . *he could have taken the letter from my purse yesterday. Jack thinks he did.*

Anyone else at Last Defense . . . *I left my purse in Jack's office when I was summoned to Michael's office by the FBI. I was gone at least twenty minutes.*

Elaine . . . *maybe Ali confided in her and she inadvertently or intentionally told someone else.*

She had to admit to herself that she wrote down Elaine's name because of the twinge of jealousy she felt over Elaine's relationship with Jack. She wondered how many times they had made love and if Elaine would try to get Jack back after she found out Jack was alive and well and as virile as ever. Would she forget about her fiancé and want to rekindle her relationship with Jack, who would probably come out as the hero in this whole affair? Lauren wondered if she could compete with Elaine for Jack's affections. Especially now, after she had mucked things up so badly by staying in Houston and letting the letter out of her possession.

Who called Ali, and why would Ali run out of his house to meet someone? While processing all the information, she put on her watch and jewelry, taking the pepper spray off the nightstand and putting it into her jean pocket.

Elaine Jones sat at the desk in her office after her conversation with Lauren. She also had an awful suspicion about the death of Ali Kasim. Her eyes filled with tears. Happy memories came to mind as she recalled the many times she'd had dinner at the Kasim house with Jack. They were an honorable family with a strong sense of duty. Now she had a bad feeling in the pit of her stomach as she considered the events of the last twenty-four hours. Last night she had planned a date with a man who was not her fiancé. She'd wanted one last night of unbridled passion before settling down to a rather mundane married life. She'd made an elaborate dinner at her house because she thought going out in public with a man other than her fiancé was not a good idea. Then, her date cancelled unexpectedly with no explanation. Now she wondered why. Did it have anything to do with the murder of Ali Kasim?

Of course not, she didn't think he would be involved in Ali's death. Besides, it was always sweeter for her to mix business and pleasure, and the sex was good. She could have mentioned it to Lauren, but she wasn't about to reveal everything to Lauren Reese. She kept her own secrets.

CHAPTER 31

In dire need of coffee and something to eat, and after pondering the recent developments about Ali Kasim, Lauren was feeling a little paranoid. Deciding to order room service instead of going down to the restaurant for breakfast, she called for a pot of coffee with cream and sugar and French toast with bacon. Immediately, she felt better.

It wasn't twenty minutes before a knock sounded at the door.

That was fast, Lauren thought. Without looking through the peephole, she opened the door.

Andy Harris stood in front of her. *How did he know I was here?*

"Hi, Andy," she said. She practically stammered, surprised and dismayed at the same time.

"Why are you here? Did you come to take me to the airport?"

"Yes, are you almost ready?"

Composing herself, she opened the door a little wider. "Oh, of course, come in. Sit down. I thought you were the breakfast I ordered. I didn't know you would be coming by."

"Go ahead and eat. I can wait. No hurry."

Andy sat down in one of the armchairs while Lauren sat in the other one. Lauren didn't feel comfortable sitting there with Andy in the small hotel room, but she had already ordered room service and the food would arrive any minute.

"So, I guess Agent Stafford is busy," Lauren said after an awkward pause. "Of course, a guy like that couldn't just drop everything and escort a woman to the airport. I'm guessing he called Last Defense and got ahold of you."

Andy looked puzzled for a brief moment and then said with a friendly smile, "That's right, I happened to be available and I wanted to see you before you left, anyway."

Another knock on the door demanded Lauren's attention. This time, it was room service. The waiter came into the room and placed the tray on the ottoman between the two chairs. Lauren signed off on the receipt, handed it back to him, and he left.

"Would you like a cup of coffee?" Lauren offered, since two cups had been delivered with breakfast.

"That would be great. I could use some coffee. I had a late night."

"Date? You did say you were seeing someone."

"No, working."

She sat down again and served up coffee for both of them. "Do you take cream or sugar?"

"No, black is fine."

"We can leave for the airport as soon as I'm done with breakfast. Believe me when I tell you, I'm ready to go home."

"I can imagine you are."

"I didn't know you were coming, or I would have been ready to leave."

"No problem. I don't mind at all. What did you do yesterday? Did you get a chance to visit anyone else while here in Houston?"

"No. Why do you ask?" Lauren said. She took a sip of her coffee.

"I was just wondering why someone as busy as you would drop everything and come to Houston. What did Jack tell you about our company that aroused your curiosity?"

"I came to check on Rick, Jack's dad, and arrange for him to continue to receive the care he's currently getting. Jack and I never talked about the company. When he came to Aspen, it was to ski and enjoy his time off. Do you mind if I eat my breakfast? Sorry to eat in front of you."

"That's perfectly all right. I've already had breakfast."

Lauren took a piece of bacon from the plate and started to eat.

"Really, Jack never mentioned anything about the company?"

"No." Lauren spoke lightly, but she was starting to get a bit concerned about the tack Andy was taking. She hoped he would stop asking about Jack and her decision to travel to Houston.

"I'm really looking forward to going back home today," she said lightly, to change the subject.

"How do you like living in Aspen?"

"It is a beautiful place. The skiing is extraordinary right now. We have a lot of champagne powder snow, and the conditions have been ideal. Do you ski?"

"I do. Well, I have in the past."

"You'll have to try Aspen."

"I'd like that."

"Just let me give you a fair warning. The planes that fly into Aspen arrive between Ajax and Highlands, down a valley. When they take off, they fly down the valley toward Glenwood Springs, and then at the last minute they push to gain altitude before going over the mountains." Lauren mimicked the planes taking off with her hands. "It's kind of scary for a lot of people."

Andy sipped his coffee. "Yes, I remember," he said.

Lauren was confused. "When we first met, you said you had never been to Aspen."

Andy looked at her, as if thinking carefully about what to say next. "I had just come in from the field that day, had lots on my mind. I didn't remember until you talked about the airport. Yeah, I guess I have been in Aspen, and I must have flown out and experienced the takeoff. You wouldn't forget a thing like that."

The phone rang and Lauren excused herself.

"Hi, I just wanted to tell you goodbye again," Jack said when Lauren answered the phone. I'm on the plane and it's starting to taxi down the runway. I wanted to tell you that I called Agent Stafford, and he's on his way to take you to the airport."

Puzzled, she asked, "Why would he come when you've sent Andy to take me to the airport?"

"I didn't send Andy to take you to the airport."

Lauren froze.

"Are you saying that Andy Harris is there—with you?" While she slowly placed the receiver back into its cradle she could hear Jack yelling into the phone, "Lauren! Lauren!"

Stunned, fear gripped her. Her heart racing, she thought about her options. Her first impulse was to run, but Andy was now standing between her and the door. Acting nonchalant, she walked calmly back to where she had been eating breakfast, a few steps away from the bathroom. Deep in thought, she analyzed each recent event and considered her options.

Andy was the head of security and knew about computers. That would give him a great deal of knowledge about hacking into phones and email. Andy probably knew that Paul was the informant Jack was working with and probably knew about the meeting they had arranged.

Oh my God. He said he was working last night.

All the pieces of the puzzle were fitting together. She was in a hotel room, alone and unprotected, with a cold-blooded killer.

Andy stood watching her closely as she picked up her coffee cup, her hand shaking. In his boyish manner, he calmly said "What's wrong? Who was on the phone?"

Lauren took a sip of coffee, dismayed when she saw how badly her hand shook.

"It was the front desk just making sure that I got my breakfast. They also asked if I wanted to reserve my seat on the shuttle. I told them you were here and would give me a ride," Lauren said, thinking quickly to come up with a credible story that would fit in with what Andy might have heard her say on the phone. The events of the last few days were beginning to fit together to make a dangerous and lethal picture. Paralyzed with fear, she thought she couldn't move. But she had to, and quickly.

"What's wrong, Lauren? The front desk has seemed to upset you," Andy said, taking a step closer to her.

"No, I'm fine."

"I would believe you, but look, you're shaking. Who was on the phone, really?"

Lauren had a fleeting memory. "You noticed the letter when everything fell from my purse inside your car. You searched for it in my purse again yesterday when I was in Michael's office."

"What letter are you talking about?"

Lauren replied in a voice not much louder than a whisper. "What was your job last night? Any job becomes . . . just a job, doesn't it? You killed Ali. Now, you've come for me."

His boyish smile vanished, and he glared at her with cold eyes. In a calm and direct voice, he spoke to her. "You killed Ali. You were partners with Jack Kelly in drug smuggling, but you got greedy, and his conscience was starting to bother him, so you killed him. Then you found out that Ali knew about you, so he had to go, too. I have plenty of evidence against you. The game is up."

Lauren stared at Andy in astonishment. "You have evidence?" she said as her mind tried to process what he had just said.

He added, "Now I just have to come up with a credible story of who would kill you."

Lauren trembled. She remembered his strong handshake and his extensive combat training. He could kill her easily if he got a hold of her. It didn't look like he had a weapon, but he wouldn't need one. When he took another step toward her, she threw her coffee at him, momentarily distracting him while he blocked the cup. The hot coffee burnt his hand, and he missed by mere inches when he tried to grab her. She was able to run into the bathroom, slam the door, and lock it. "Why?" she screamed.

"What do you want me to say?" Andy shouted through the barrier of the door. "Do you think I'm fighting on one side or the other? There are no sides. I did it for the same reason that everyone else at Last Defense does, but won't admit it. I did it for the money."

Andy wrenched the door with no success. Lauren watched in fear. The knob rattled again, then she sprang backward as he rammed the door with his entire weight. "Unlike your new boyfriend," he said, his breathing heavy, "I never trusted you."

New boyfriend? He must mean Michael, Lauren thought. *Is Michael in on this?* Her thoughts went back to when she'd interrupted them talking in Michael's office. Right before Andy took her sightseeing.

"You came here to snoop around, just like your Aspen lover. You idiots never learn to mind your own business."

Again, Andy rammed the door, and Lauren thought that he was going to break it down. She wanted to distract him while she had a chance to think. If she stalled, maybe someone would hear the commotion and call hotel security or the police.

"What about Omar? Why him?" she shouted through the door.

"Hasn't your new boyfriend told you about collateral damage?"

"The FBI is on the way. They know you're here. You'll never get away."

"According to my computer log in, I'm not here. Just like I was never in Aspen. Don't you just love technology? And you won't be alive to tell anyone that I ever was here."

"Room service saw you."

"I made sure he didn't. Anyway, he was more interested in catching a glimpse of what was down your blouse, than who was in the room with you."

Lauren looked around. *I am not going to die in this bathroom. There's got to be something I can do.* With a flash of insight, she remembered the pepper spray in her pocket and took it out. *The lock isn't going to hold much longer. It's now or never.* She could see the door jamb starting to give way.

Quickly unlocking the door, she wrenched it open and forcefully sprayed Andy in the face. She held her breath and prayed, knowing this was her only chance to escape.

Andy's quick reflexes allowed him to dodge most of the pepper spray, but not all. He flew backward, gasping for air, bent at the waist and coughing, his hands tearing at his eyes. That gave Lauren enough time to run to the front door and into the hallway, to freedom.

She had held her breath to avoid inhaling the pepper spray, but that wasn't enough. Choking and gasping for air, she ran toward the stairwell. She paused on the second floor to catch her breath, when she heard Andy in pursuit. Again, she found the strength to run down the two final flights of stairs and burst into the lobby.

Agent Stafford stood by the front desk wearing a dark blue jacket with FBI printed on the back. He was talking on a cell phone. Eyes burning and out of breath, Lauren ran toward him. He quickly pocketed his phone and met her halfway. "More agents are on the way," he assured her. She pointed to the stairwell. "He's in there," she managed to say, just before she collapsed in his arms.

As Agent Stafford attended to Lauren, his relief backup, Agent Chris Thomas, quickly headed toward the stairwell. Before he got there, Andy rushed out, barreling through a group of hotel guests, then ran out into the back parking lot of the hotel. An ambush of officers from several agencies were waiting for him, guns drawn. Andy skidded to a halt, and his hands shot up above his head. "I'm unarmed," he yelled as Agent Thomas approached him from behind, grabbing his wrists and slamming him against one of the police cars.

"This is just a domestic dispute. She's crazy," Andy screamed as Thomas frisked and cuffed him. "She asked me to take her to the airport and then she went off and sprayed me with pepper spray. I tell you, she's crazy!"

CHAPTER 32

In Aspen, the next day, Lauren walked toward David Richards' office apprehensively. He'd told her not to come into work. But, after her ordeal, she'd been treated and released from the hospital, had given her statement to the authorities, and had still made the arranged flights to Denver and Aspen. She was anxious to get home, sleep in her own bed and return to a normal life.

She'd rehearsed how to apologize and explain her decision to travel to Houston, knowing that Jack Kelly was not on the missing plane. She was sure that David had been filled in about everything by now and knew the entire story. Standing at the closed door of his office, she took a deep breath, opened the door and walked in. Much to her surprise, David was happy, almost giddy, to see her. He didn't seem angry at all.

"Hi, Lauren. Have a seat. You didn't have to come in today after the dreadful day you had yesterday."

Sitting down in the guest chair with her hands in her lap, she said, "David, I want to apologize and explain . . ."

"No need to explain. I've been filled in. You're a brave woman."

"Thank you."

"I didn't know you were involved in international crime and there was no reason to tell me. You brought an end to this investigation. The mystery of the sabotaged plane has been solved, thanks to you. We can now go back to normal operations. Just in time. We're due for another snow storm and it looks like we still have many more months of a great ski season."

"I heard that you were interviewed several times by the NTSB."

"Well, they weren't too hard on me," David said. "Just doing their job. Actually, they recommended to my superiors that I take a month off after ski season to spend some time with my family. The airport is giving me an all-expense-paid trip to Hawaii. How great is that?"

"That's wonderful. You truly deserve it."

"Good to have you back, Lauren."

"It's good to be back."

"And Jack?"

"He's in Afghanistan right now. I'm waiting to hear from him."

"You've inspired me. If you and Jack can reconnect after twelve years, I figure my wife and I can, too. We've not been communicating with each other for a number of years—even though we've been living in the same house." He laughed.

Lauren smiled, but David could see a questioning look in her eyes.

"I know there have been rumors. I don't know if I can get my marriage back, but I'm sure going to try."

"I'm sure you can," Lauren said. "By the way, I heard that you knew Jennifer Summers, one of the passengers aboard the downed plane. I didn't realize she was a friend, or I would have said something when I called you earlier. I'm so sorry."

David's expression turned to one of sadness and grief. "It did hit me hard," he said as he stared out the window. "But it made me appreciate the people that are important to me. Life is so fragile. We need to hold on to those we love and connect with them on every level. We should always tell them how we feel about them and never let them slip away from us. Jennifer will be missed by many friends and co-workers."

"My sympathies—for the loss of your friend."

"Thanks," David said. Then, after a quiet pause and looking at his desk, overrun with papers and message slips, he said, "I guess I need to get back to work. Welcome home, Lauren. We missed you around here."

"I missed you too. It's good to be home."

CHAPTER 33

Six months later—Aspen, Colorado

Lauren slipped into her nontraditional bridal dress, the dress she'd always dreamed she'd wear for this special day. In her bedroom, she sat at her antique dresser putting on her earrings when he walked in. She saw him in the mirror. He looked handsome, dressed in a black tuxedo with a red rose boutonniere.

"How did you get past security?" Lauren asked, referring to her sister Shannon, who was in the living room coordinating the final arrangements for the wedding.

"It wasn't easy. I had to use some diversion techniques I learned while in the field." Michael Dodson said, smiling. "You look beautiful."

Lauren smiled back, "Thank you."

"Look, I bought you a present," Michael said as he handed her a box wrapped in red tissue.

Lauren opened her gift and laughed. Pepper spray. "Thanks, you shouldn't have," she said as she set the box beside a bottle of perfume on the dresser.

"I thought you might need it for the honeymoon."

Lauren laughed again.

"Are you sure you want to go through with this? It's not too late to back out."

"Yes, I'm sure," Lauren beamed.

"May I kiss the bride?"

"Sure."

He stood behind her, bent down, and kissed her neck. Pausing, she gazed up at him briefly before turning back to the mirror and putting on her pearl necklace.

Looking at her reflection, he said, "These last six months seem like a bad dream. We've gone through a lot."

"Yes, it was a tough time," Lauren agreed, suddenly turning serious as she remembered the ordeal.

"I guess it was all about trust. Omar didn't know whom to trust, and that's what got him killed. We became so reliant on our technology that we forgot awareness. We never suspected that the computer program was giving us faulty Intel."

"Did you really think a computer program could measure what's in a person's heart and mind?"

"No, only a woman can do that," Michael smiled. He continued, "You can tell us whom to hire from now on. Joe said you were cleared. Of course, you haven't gone through the background check yet or the extensive physical."

"Let me guess. You give the physical, right?"

"Well, yes. How'd you know? But more importantly, rumor has it that the FBI has a file on you—for lying to an agent. That's serious business, you know."

"That's been cleared up. We're all friends now. I invited Agent Stafford to the wedding. Hope you're okay with that."

Ignoring the last comment, Michael said, "Andy configured the computer program to give us the intelligence that he wanted us to have. It was one of his many ways of manipulation. He got away with his lucrative drug trafficking business for years, working both sides. Playing on our prejudices and fears, he always knew exactly what to say. And he must have kept a database to track all the lies he was telling us."

"Did Andy somehow manipulate the situation that called Jack to Afghanistan?"

"No, Jack went on his own, trusting the intelligence from the report that Paul had received from Omar. We both ended up in Afghanistan to find out what was going on, both of us suspecting the other for different reasons."

"What was your involvement with Colonel Shore?"

"We were working on a sting operation to find out if any U.S. servicemen or any of our own guys were involved in smuggling heroin and opiates out of the country."

"What happened?"

"I got caught up in working on industry standard changes in D.C. and put Andy in charge of the operation. It was like putting the fox in charge of the hen house."

Lauren stood up and faced Michael. "That's pretty scary," she said.

"Now Jack, he knows the true meaning of trust," Michael said as he reached out and held Lauren's hand.

"What do you mean?"

"He trusted me to pick you up and bring you to the church."

"Can you be trusted?" she teased.

"I guess we'll see," he said with a smile. "Jack is a lucky guy."

"Thanks. And you. I figured out that it was all about honor with you. You didn't want to admit that you could have slipped up, which kept you from acting on your suspicions about Andy," Lauren said thoughtfully.

"Your right-hand man that you trusted with your life went rogue. But you finally did admit it and I respect you for that. If Jack hadn't been in the picture—who knows what would've happened between us?"

"I'd have a chance with you?"

"Of course. You knew I was a bit smitten with you. Your charm is mesmerizing."

"You're really testing this trust and honor thing, aren't you?"

203

Lauren laughed and hit him playfully with her bouquet. "Take me to the church. Now!"

On the way to the church, Michael remembered the day Lauren had almost become another one of Andy Harris's victims. He had arrived in Afghanistan late in the afternoon and was meeting again with Army Colonel Shore in his office on the outskirts of a military compound. Shore was still investigating someone he knew as Mr. X on suspicions of working with a tribal drug lord distributing heroin, morphine, and other opiates among U.S. soldiers. Eight soldiers had died of drug overdoses in the last few years. His sting operation, conducted outside proper channels and set up with Michael Dodson and other contractors, had turned up nothing.

It was a somber reality. The illicit drug trade in the war zone resulted in young Afghans peddling heroin, soldiers dying after mixing opiates, troops stealing from medical bags, Afghan soldiers and police dealing drugs to their U.S. comrades.

"You said that you had some surveillance video that you wanted me to see," Michael told Shore. "I'm sorry that I didn't come here sooner."

"I'm just glad you're here now," Shore said as he stepped to his computer and turned the monitor toward Michael. "The picture's a little grainy and hard to see, but I was hoping you might be able to recognize who this is in the video. It was taken a few months ago from a drop-off exchange outside Herat."

"So this is a place where you're certain drugs were being exchanged for cash or weapons?"

"That's correct," Shore said as he pointed to a few of the Afghan locals, "We know these guys here are working for the drug lord. Can you recognize the American they're dealing with?"

Michael studied the video. Stunned, he said, "Yes, that's Andy Harris."

Colonel Shore was ecstatic. Finally he was able to put a name to the face that he had for so long tried to identify—the face of

Mr. X. Just then, his cell phone rang. Irritated, Shore answered the call.

Michael walked calmly over to the window and put his face in his hands. *How long has this been going on?*

After a brief conversation, Shore ended the call. "We've both been summoned to Army Criminal Investigation Command," he said. "Why don't you drive? You have a nicer vehicle."

The Humvee tore through the destitute area where Colonel Shore's office was located—to the offices of the Army Command about forty minutes away. When they arrived, a soldier armed with a rifle came out to escort them into the building. To Michael's surprise, he found Jack Kelly in the commander's office, along with a CIA agent. Keeping a calm demeanor about him, he sat down in a guest chair and took a deep breath.

He turned to Jack first. "So, Jack, you've decided to join the living after all," Michael said in a clipped voice. "And exactly what have you done with Lauren?"

"Lauren is in a safe place, no thanks to you," Jack said wryly, his feelings for her showing in his face and the tone of his voice. "She's been a good friend to me, and your plan to hide her away didn't work very well. What exactly were your intentions? Did you know that by keeping her in Houston another day, she was almost killed!"

"Oh my God, you're serious, aren't you? Is she okay? Tell me what's going on."

Jack relayed how he had avoided the plane crash and how he'd come to be working with Lauren who'd volunteered to meet with Paul Johnson in Houston. He explained all that he had learned in the last few days, and when he described the events that happened earlier with Lauren and Andy, Michael felt the blood drain out of his face.

"I just found out about Andy myself," Michael said. "I recognized him in a surveillance video that Colonel Shore just showed me. It's quite a shock. I had no idea."

Another agent piped in. "We believe that Mr. Harris arranged the ambush that killed Omar Kasim. We suspect he shot Omar's father, Ali Kasim and are investigating him in connection with a plane crash in Aspen."

"Is Andy in custody now?" Michael asked.

"Yes, but of course, he's denying everything and demanding to see a lawyer."

"What was your part in this, Mr. Dodson?" the agent asked.

"I had absolutely no connection with Omar's death or with anything that Andy was doing illegally," Michael insisted. "You can inspect any records, any phone calls, and any plane trips I've taken. The only thing I'm guilty of is being duped by Andy—as you were too, Jack." Michael looked directly into his eyes.

"I have to admit that I was taken in by him, too," Jack said. "He had an ingenious plan to protect his innocence, while getting us all to turn on each other."

They focused the remainder of the meeting on how to arrest the other conspirators in Andy's lucrative drug smuggling business. They also discussed what procedures could now be put into place to keep an eye on the scattered U.S. Military's troops and private contractors serving in a country awash with poppy fields that provide up to 90 percent of the world's opium.

At the end of the session, Jack asked to talk to Michael privately.

"Michael, you and I go back a long way. We've been through a lot together, and I hope we can put this behind us, now that we've found out the truth."

"You should know that my intentions with Lauren were completely honorable," Michael said.

"My plan was to keep her safe at my house. I also thought that if there was any way to bring you to Houston, and out of hiding, it would be to stop Lauren from reporting in to you on her cell phone. I also wanted to find out the truth. Andy convinced us all that you arranged for Omar's transfer to where he was ambushed. That was why I suspected you."

"I didn't transfer Omar, and I was surprised to hear where Omar was when he was killed. I thought that you sent him there. So, I also had reasons to suspect you. We both should have confided in each other."

"Yes, we should have," Michael agreed. "Andy played us for fools."

"Until this mess is cleared up," Jack said, "I'm taking a leave of absence from Last Defense, if that's what you want to call it."

"I understand."

With that, Jack walked out, leaving Michael deflated from the revelations of the day.

CHAPTER 34

With the wedding service about to begin in the quaint Aspen church, the guests sat reverently, listening to the organ music being played. Lauren's friends and coworkers had arrived, along with some of Jack's college friends that he had known throughout the years. The sun shone through the stained glass windows, and a perfectly arranged mixture of fresh red and white roses and spring lilies adorned the church.

Jack looked handsome in his black tux. Gone were any traces of the stressed-out appearance he had worn when Lauren had first seen him at the Aspen airport six months ago. Jack had flown his dad and the disabled man's caregiver in on a private charter from Houston. Eric Reese, Lauren's cousin, was so happy to see his former mentor that he hugged Rick, and, later he swore he saw a hint of recognition in Rick's eyes. After all, how could anyone forget Eric? Eric's parents beamed with happiness as they also welcomed old friends.

At Lauren's suggestion, Michael Dodson served as best man. Lauren thought Jack and Michael should forgive each other, and having Michael as best man would serve as an act of reconciliation. But first, she had to convince Jack that Michael's intentions had been honorable that day he had taken her to his house. Jack was worried that her affections were with Michael instead of him, so she'd done her best to prove him wrong. No one but Jack had a piece of her heart. He made her laugh and feel safe and content.

Lauren had asked her sister, Shannon, to be her maid of honor. Shannon's husband Bill was also in the wedding party, as well as their two children who filled the role of flower girl and ring bearer. It had been a happy and friendly group, as they waited to share the joy of a wedding that had been a long time coming.

Lauren wore a white French taffeta knee length dress, awash in inky roses on a shimmering background. The vintage silhouette finished with a pleated scoop neck, gathered straps and a high cummerbund waist that released to a soft pleated skirt. Glammed up with sparkling drop earrings, a pearl necklace and stretch bead bracelets, Lauren caught the eye of all the guests who stood as she walked down the aisle. Small white flowers graced her upswept hair, and she carried a bouquet of red and white roses that matched the flower arrangements in the church. In an unconventional move, Jack stepped down from the stairs and held his hand out to Lauren when she'd almost reached the end of the aisle.

The memory of international crime had faded, and the hope of new beginnings filled the church with a warm glow. Jack had resigned from Last Defense but had remained friends with Michael Dodson, who was cleared of all knowledge and complicity relating to the illegal activities of Andy Harris. Michael had admitted that he had lost focus. He'd given Andy too much control over the operations side of the business during the month's he'd been concentrating on marketing.

Andy Harris was awaiting trial for numerous crimes, including the murder of Omar and Ali Kasim and the attempted murder of Lauren. Investigators determined from forensic evidence of the bomb material that they also had enough evidence to charge Andy with the plane crash in Aspen. The passengers had merely been in the wrong place at the wrong time. The investigators, along with the President of the United States and all U.S. government high ranking officials had been relieved that the Saudi national was not the intended victim.

Jack accepted a Chief Financial Officer position with a company in Denver who held contracts with the Department of Homeland Security, and, together, he and Lauren moved back to the big city, bringing his dad with him. Lauren had already found a facility that specialized in dementia patients so that his dad could receive the best of care and where the newly married couple could visit often. Since Lauren would be moving back to Denver, her wedding day was bittersweet. She would miss her many friends and coworkers at the airport in Aspen.

CHAPTER 35

Lauren looked at the man she was sharing wedding vows with. She thought about the last six months and remembered what had convinced her to marry Jack. At his invitation, she had arrived in Houston for a visit shortly after he returned from Afghanistan.

Jack's luxury condominium had been furnished by a professional interior decorator. Still, the place looked barely lived in.

"Please, make yourself at home," Jack had said as he took off his jacket and motioned for her to take a seat on the white leather couch in the living room. "Would you like anything to drink?"

"A glass of water would be good."

"Great. That's the one thing I do have," he said.

Lauren sat down on the couch and took off her sweater while Jack went to get the water.

"I'm so glad you've come to visit me in Houston," Jack said, handing her the glass. "At this point, I wouldn't blame you if you never wanted to see me again after getting you involved in that mess, not to mention what you went through the last day you were here."

"I volunteered, remember? You didn't force me, or even ask me to do anything I didn't want to do."

"Well, I admit you were able to take care of yourself pretty well, with your pepper spray and all." He smiled. "I'll never mess with you," he teased as he sat down next to her on the couch.

Lauren smiled back. "Maybe this could be the start of something good. When consciences collide with crash landings, everything doesn't have to end up negatively, does it?"

"No, it doesn't." He snuggled up to her and gently touched her warm face with his hand.

"I was so jealous of Michael," he admitted. "The thought of you and Michael brought out feelings in me that I didn't know I had and your house in Aspen isn't the same without you in it. I couldn't sit still there another minute. I had to get to Houston. Luckily, I'd heard from Paul and left early Wednesday morning.

"Michael was very charming and exciting. But he's not my type," Lauren assured him.

"I'm very happy to hear that. And Elaine is definitely not my type," Jack confessed with a Cheshire-cat smile on his face.

"How do you know that I went to see Elaine?" Lauren asked.

"After word had leaked that I was very much alive, she tracked me down and told me. She also wanted to know the status of the relationship between you and me, realizing we were more than friends. She didn't waste any time letting me know that she would reconsider her engagement if I wanted to get back together with her. I told her to forget it."

Lauren couldn't hide a relieved smile as she said, "I have to admit, I was a little jealous of Elaine also. Who is she engaged to?"

"Some hedge fund manager, older than her and not the type she usually goes for, but rich enough to keep her happy and I've heard he's a good guy. Actually, she could use a little stability so it's probably not a bad match. She needs to settle down."

"I can't believe she came on to you, after all of this and the situation with her nephew."

"I heard Ken is getting help with his gambling addiction. I guess you could say he was scared straight. He has a wife and a small child. Last Defense hired him back, but I'm sure they're watching him closely. I think he's on the right track now."

"They hired him back? I wonder how Elaine managed that. I still have suspicions about her. I had told her on the phone that I was at the Marriott shortly before Andy showed up."

"You're probably wondering how Andy found out you were there, right? I've wondered about that myself. It's possible that Andy called her right after she spoke with you and she innocently told him where you were. They had a tight relationship, and he probably got a lot of information from her. That would also account for how Andy found out about Ken's blackmail scheme and knew Ken was the culprit when he received his letter. Andy nipped that in the bud—scared Ken into hiding. Maybe that was the jolt Ken needed to go straight, to stop gambling and become a responsible family man."

"You're guessing, Jack. Elaine, on the other hand, might have called Andy right away and told him where I was. Now who's protecting people they like?" Jack laughed too, and blushed slightly. "Andy could have also just called every airport hotel in Houston. It wouldn't have been that hard to find you. You were registered under your own name. What were we thinking? We've been accustomed to turning to technology for everything. Sometimes, you can just pick up the phone."

"I guess that's possible. Do you think Elaine was sleeping with Andy?"

"Yeah. After she and I broke up, I did hear a rumor that they hooked up. I think she was using Andy to make me jealous, and he was using her for information. It was a perfect codependent relationship, with benefits."

"How nice."

"Women seemed to go for Andy, his boyish looks and charm. Not to mention his six-pack abs. His credentials were top-notch. It was hard to suspect him, and no one ever did. If I had been on the plane that left Aspen, and been killed, Andy had manufactured enough evidence to frame me for the drug smuggling that Omar had written about in his report. Since Paul had a copy of the report, it would have come out eventually. Andy had to get rid of me to make the evidence stick.

"Do you think Elaine knew what Andy was doing?"

"No, I don't think she had anything to do with his illegal activities or was at all aware of them. And I'm not just saying that to protect her. She could have become collateral damage, herself, if she would have found out much more about the case. Andy tried to convince her that I was Mr. X but he underestimated her feelings for me. She wasn't buying it."

"I guess you're right. She was in danger and didn't realize it. When Michael and I were in her office, she did seem very upset about Omar, and also about Ali when I talked to her later. I don't think she could have faked that. So, I believe you, you've convinced me that she was not involved."

"I never suspected her. She's a little shallow . . ."

"A little?" Lauren interrupted.

Jack gave Lauren a disapproving look and continued. "Elaine's a little shallow and she has her faults, but basically she's a good person."

"And when it comes to you, I can't fault her taste in men."

Jack put his arms around Lauren as he said, "I would have to say that Michael has excellent taste in women as well. I think his magnetism had a lot to do with why you wanted to stay in Houston."

"No, it wasn't him. I wanted to meet with Ali. His letter was vague and if you read it a certain way, it seemed like he was suggesting you were responsible for the death of Omar. I realize now that it doesn't say that."

"I think your imagination was getting the best of you."

"I just needed time to try to unravel everything in my mind. Michael was implicating you and making a pretty good case—you missing the plane and becoming very secretive and evasive. When

I was told that you had Omar sent to Faizabad, it didn't look good for you. I guess I was afraid to come home before I knew the truth."

"I didn't have Omar transferred there. Andy did. He forged my signature on the transfer papers. There was a lot of insurgent activity in that area, and we did have personnel there. Since I was in charge of operations, no one questioned the forged documents. By that point Andy was getting desperate. He knew Omar had suspicions and figured it was just a matter of time before Omar confided them directly to me or Michael."

"Do you think Omar would have?"

"No. I think Omar just wanted to complete his contract and go home. He was done. Paul had been pulled out of Afghanistan for a different assignment and had to turn his attentions to his new job. Omar probably thought no one really cared about his report."

"Elaine said that Omar turned in his report to his supervisor, George Kaye."

"Yes, but George then turned it over to Andy who told George to keep it top secret, that he would handle it. Then Andy promoted George to another position in another area. Omar's detailed report must have implicated Andy in a way that Omar himself wasn't even aware of."

"I wonder if Omar told his dad about his report."

"That would be my guess. However, Ali realized Andy killed his son when he remembered something Omar had told him. Andy had been a sharpshooter, of extraordinary ability. That was the piece of the puzzle that no one else had. That information should have been in Andy's personnel file but it was deleted, I'd guess, by Andy himself. I don't know how Omar knew about it."

"What a terrible waste of a talented young man with such a promising future ahead of him."

"Your arrival in Houston brought everything out of the shadows. I could never have done it without you, Lauren. As I mentioned, Andy was going to eliminate me and provide evidence that I was Mr. X. He must have been flabbergasted when you showed up. Then he quickly had to come up with a scenario to frame you. You were instrumental in bringing Andy to justice, pressing on with the investigation from an outsider's perspective. I only wish you'd left when I told you to. I knew you were in grave danger, and I was worried sick about your safety. That's why I never told you that Paul had contacted me. I wanted you to drop your inquiries and leave Houston, but I guess I was too late. Once you'd met Michael and others at Last Defense you were caught in their web. I wasn't sure how to get you out."

"I know," Lauren said.

"Andy is a sociopathic manipulator. His position in the company, his background in security technology, and his impressive combat skills in the field proved to be a lethal combination—which allowed him to start his own lucrative heroin trafficking business. Before long, he began to believe he was beyond the reach of the law."

"Did Michael ever suspect Andy?"

"He finally did, which is why he never told Andy about the FBI or about taking you to his home, even though Andy asked where you were. Michael had a vague recollection that Andy was a sniper but couldn't find confirmation in his personnel file."

"I guess Michael's in the clear, then," Lauren said, thoughtfully.

"When Andy got hold of the letter that Ali had written to me, he realized Ali had to be eliminated or his house-of-cards would tumble down."

"I wonder what Andy told Ali to lure him out of his home."

"I have no idea. I've often wondered that myself."

"Did you go to Ali's funeral?"

"Yes, it was packed. He was loved and respected throughout the community."

Lauren became subdued when she thought about Omar and Ali.

Jack changed the subject.

"Why didn't you tell me that you went to see Elaine?"

"I didn't want you to know that I was spying on you. It seemed like everyone was trying to implicate you as the killer," she said. "I don't think you understand the kind of pressure I was under."

"I do understand, but . . . you are an exceptional woman, Lauren."

"Are you just figuring that out now?"

"No, I figured that out a long time ago." He stole a kiss and pushed to his feet. "And I can prove it."

"Really?"

"That's one of the reasons I brought you here. There's something I want to show you."

Jack went into the storage closet of his bedroom. Lauren heard him shuffling around for a few minutes, before he came back with a letter in his hand. *Return to Sender* had been clearly stamped on the face of the envelope, even though it had been addressed correctly to her home in Aspen.

"Can I open it?" Lauren asked.

"It's addressed to you, isn't it?"

Excited, Lauren opened the letter and, to her surprise, it contained heartfelt words expressing his feelings for her and asking if they could continue their relationship, if necessary by long distance, until they could figure out a way to be together. Lauren wondered what her life would have been like if she had received the letter at the time it had been mailed, over ten years ago.

Of course, you can't change the past. Lauren held back tears. Seeing the letter was what she'd needed to believe in Jack. It confirmed that he was sincere about the feelings he'd had about her long ago and, hopefully, still had. Now she understood why he thought she had moved on. She had never reached out to him, either. A simple lack of communication came between them. But the past was the past.

"As you know, I've resigned from Last Defense," Jack said as he gently took Lauren's hand.

"I can't say that I blame you, after all that has happened."

"Still, leaving the company that I helped create was a hard thing to do."

"What are you going to do now?"

"I've been looking at a variety of other options. A few companies are interested in me, and I've been on several interviews. I want to try something a little different. I don't think I'm cut out for private security contracting. It's a tough business where you're always walking a fine line."

"I can understand that," Lauren said. "Are you going to stay in Houston?"

"Well, the skiing is not that great here." Jack laughed. "Actually, I've been looking in Colorado." Jack gently kissed Lauren on the nape of her neck. "I think it's time for this guy to go back home."

He found her mouth, and Lauren slipped her arms around him. Locked in a passionate embrace, Jack said, "My parents aren't coming home tonight," he joked. "Would you like to move to the bedroom?"

Between kisses and laughter, Lauren managed to say, "Yes, I would. I've wanted you for such a long time . . . again."

"Me, too," Jack said with a deep smile of satisfaction.

They drew apart long enough for Jack to carry her to his bed. There she once again found the man who'd held and caressed her with such tenderness years ago. As Jack took off his shirt, Lauren flashed back to her house in Aspen where he had worn no shirt on the day after the plane went missing. In her mind's eye she pictured him waiting to launder his clothes. She had secretly hoped she would see him without his shirt again, but this time she wanted to be able to run her fingers along the muscles of his tight chest. Did he realize how deeply she wanted him? She began to fulfill her fantasy.

"Your turn," Jack said as he helped Lauren unbutton her blouse. She took off her blouse and bra and let herself fall back on the bed, pulling him with her. He again found her mouth with his, as his gentle hands caressed her breasts. Their kisses were deep and urgent, familiar and full of longing, for it had seemed like an eternity since they had seen each other at the Aspen airport. Their yearning for the carnal knowledge they had once known so well sparked between them. Crushing her so tightly against his chest that she could barely breathe, he said, "Marry me."

Lauren hadn't expected this proposal. She breathlessly managed to say, "You're trouble."

"I know," he said as he nibbled her neck. "But you love trouble."

She slid off the rest of her clothes, and within what seemed liked seconds, Jack had his pants off. Unable to conceal his desire for her, he drew her close. She felt his heart beating with excitement, matching the beat of her own, and all the tension of the previous few months melted away as they became swept up in passion.

Deep inside her heart, she knew Jack was always the right man for her. She hoped that this time, consummating their relationship would be the beginning of a bright future together.

Jack formalized his marriage proposal a few months later, when he came to Denver for his new job. He told her he would be in Aspen, and asked if she would like to go to dinner with him. Lauren had been pleasantly surprised when she realized Jack had invited Shannon and her family to join them.

Jack dazzled Lauren with a gorgeous engagement ring that he placed on her plate when she stepped away from the table before dessert. Lauren's niece and nephew giggled, watching Lauren with big eyes of anticipation as she came back to the table.

She'd known in her heart why Jack had decided to come back to Aspen. Ski season was ending, so he was coming to see her, anxious to start his new life in Colorado. She knew he'd had offers in other cities and other areas of the country, but he'd held out for Denver.

When she formally accepted his marriage proposal, Jack said, "I told you that I would win you back."

The restaurant gifted champagne to celebrate the occasion, as the owner knew Lauren and thought of her as a friend, remembering the many times she had helped him with his own travel arrangements.

CHAPTER 36

After the brief wedding ceremony, all the guests exited the church and headed over to the historic Hotel Jerome for the dinner and reception. Michael toasted the bride and groom with sincere wishes for a happy life together.

Lauren hugged and thanked her sister for planning the perfect wedding. "I always knew in my heart that you and Jack were right for each other," Shannon affirmed.

Lauren looked at her boss, David Richards, and wondered if she would ever again work for such a wonderful man. It seemed as though he and his wife had rekindled the fire in their marriage. They appeared very happy together. Tears flowed as Lauren said her goodbyes. She knew she would miss all her colleagues at the airport.

Back in Houston, Joseph Chen entered information about Lauren and Jack into his computer. The program confirmed his own suspicions that the marriage of Jack and Lauren would never last. He smiled as he closed his laptop. *What a foolish chance they are taking.* Then he reminded himself that he was single, unattached, and going home to an empty house every night. He thought about Kate and picked up his phone to give her a call. Something he had meant to do many times in the last few months. This time, he actually did make the connection. It was time for him to take a foolish chance.

The wedding guests talked and mingled at the Hotel Jerome, enjoying the fine food and drink as they celebrated Jack and Lauren's marriage. They all knew that in this room there was an abundance of trust, honor, integrity, and love.

No computers.

THE AUTHOR

Born and raised in Denver, Colorado, Joan Carson-Schoepflin is an alumna of Colorado University at Denver with two career passions, writing mysteries and accounting. She also hosts and produces murder mystery parties with her brother. She is currently working on her next mystery novel.